PLACES

OF

REFUGE

PLACES OF REFUGE

MICHAEL ALLEN GEORGE

ARPress
45 Dan Road Suite 5
Canton MA 02021

Hotline: 1(888) 821-0229
Fax: 1(508) 545-7580

Ordering Information:
Quantity sales. Special discounts are available on quantity purchases by corporations, associations, and others. For details, contact the publisher at the address above.

Printed in the United States of America.

ISBN-13: Softcover   979-8-89356-476-1
              eBook   979-8-89356-475-4

Library of Congress Control Number: 2024904596

Contents

Dedicated to

My wife

Marilynn Ruth George

Thank you for 55 years of great memories.
With you gone, I cherish them
And the love always there
Through our lifetime together

Book By
Michael Allen George

The Refuge Mystery Series

Other books by Michael Allen George

Horses Lemons And Pretty Girls
More Horses And Pretty Girls
Finding Peri Gray
Of Rain Barrels And Bridges

Books written with
Bud George and David George

Stories From Three Brothers
More Stories From Three Brothers

Prologue

They drove deep into the refuge. Three men. One driving, the other two roughly moving their hands over the near nude, tightly bound young girl riding between them.

They parked on a grassy hillside, dragged her out of the car, and laid her down on brittle dry grass. They kept the gag on her mouth and the ties on her wrists. They untied her legs and spread them.

The biggest of the three men lifted her skirt up, over her waist, and slowly pulled off her panties. He delighted in watching the terror slowly creep over her face. This was his supreme joy. Nothing in life filled him fuller than did torturing, then raping a woman. Especially one this young.

The three were always on the lookout for someone they could grab and use for their sick satisfaction, but finding this one was pure luck for them.

They were filling the tank on their car when she pulled in. She skipped the pumps and went inside. One of the men moved close behind her car and waited for her.

It was an older service station, with a dimly lit drive, so he stood in the shadows. She came out with a gallon of milk and a small bag of groceries. The man behind her car moved quickly when she tried to open her car door. He grabbed her, slapped one hand over her mouth, and before she had a chance to try to wrestle free, the other two men were on her.

They dragged her to their car and into the backseat. They put her milk and groceries onto the floor in back by her feet. Two of the men joined her on the seat with her. They quickly tied her as the driver sped out of the station. It would be a couple of hours before the man inside the station realized her car was still there.

"Where are we going with her?" One of the men in the back asked.

"Damned if I know," answered the driver of the car.

"Let's not fool around," said the third man. "Let's take her into the refuge."

"Good idea," said the first man. "It's close enough."

They tore at her clothes as they rode, anxious to get their hands on her. Now, with her on the ground two of the men took pleasure in watching the big man take her. They found it exciting to watch her squirm and try to pull away as he did.

He was too strong, and she had no chance in succeeding. She had no chance with the other two either. By the time the big man finished, she was so battered and beaten she had no fight left.

When the third man took her, he was allowed his own supreme joy. It was his turn, and he delighted in taking it. Just as he was reaching his moment, he wrapped his hands around her neck and squeezed. His timing was good, and she died just as he climaxed.

"By god," he said rather loudly, "I love it when it works like that. Seein' them go just when I do, is the greatest feeling."

"We know that," said the big guy. "Now what should we do with her?"

"Bury her like always. There's plenty places here."

"You gonna dig the hole? Cause I ain't in the mood."

"I got a better idea. Let's burn the body. Won't no one be the wiser. It ain't likely anyone will be back here for a long time."

"How we gonna do that? What're we gonna use to burn her."

"We got that can a gas in the trunk. That should do it."

"Good idea."

They poured the full two gallons of gas over her, with some on the ground around her. They didn't expect the reaction they got when they lit it. Not only the gas went up in flames. No more than an instant went by before the dry, brittle grass went up too.

The flames in the grass were followed by those in a nearby stand of extremely dry pines. They were in full flames before the three men escaped the refuge. The blaze was totally out of control within an hour.

As the fire raged, the slight breeze grew stronger, further pushing the flames. By the time the fire was called in, the chances of controlling it were slim. Before the first crews got there, putting the fire out wasn't going to happen.

All they could do was hope to control it enough to keep it from spreading onto any neighbors land. Before morning, flames were reaching as high as a hundred feet. The crackling of the fire could be heard a fair distance, and the flames seen for miles.

It was a fire that would have an effect on many people in many ways. That included the three very stupid, evil and totally useless men who started it. Men who were now trembling in fear from the thought of what would have happened to them had they not escaped the refuge.

CHAPTER 1

The smell woke Dave Sanders up. He struggled to open his eyes. The crackling sound got him out of bed, if sitting up on the edge of the bed is getting out of it. He was anxious to get up and moving, to see what was making the smoke. All he needed to do was convince his body to move.

If it was outside, where he fervently hoped it was, it had to be a powerful fire. Elaine answered his question, without speaking to him.

"Relax, Jill," she said softly, from the room across the hall, "the fire's outside."

She was trying to sooth Jill's nerves. She was agitated from the smell of smoke, almost strong enough to be coming from a fire inside the house.

Dave pushed his stiff, unyielding muscles enough to stand. He turned around so he was facing them. Elaine was doing her best to take off Jill's pajamas.

"Do you know, Elaine," he asked, "where the fire is? I think it must be a big one."

"No idea. Why don't you go out and look?"

He wore sweats to bed, so he was already dressed well enough to go outside. Not that it mattered much, living in the country the way they did.

"Have you looked outside yet?" he asked her.

"Not yet. Jill needed the potty right away, so I haven't had the chance."

Elaine was struggling to put a fresh diaper and pants on her. He would have offered to help, but knew he'd only get in the way. It was a task that didn't work as well with two doing it as it did with only one. And with Jill now sleeping on a hospital bed, assisting her was easier with all the electrical adjustments the bed provided.

"I'm going out to take a look then," he said.

"We'll be right behind you," she answered.

He pushed his feet into his moccasin type slippers and went outside.

The sight when Dave got there filled him with dread, but also a sense of wonder. The fire was obviously out of control. The red/orange flames danced nearly a hundred feet in the air, and they were no doubt headed their way. It was easy to see that if they got much closer, it would be time to evacuate. Something he didn't want to do. Taking Jill anywhere was never easy. Taking her under these circumstances was going to be a hassle at best. And, of course, he didn't want to leave their home vacant. There was too much chance of it being vandalized if the fire never reached it.

It looked as though the whole of the wildlife refuge was burning, which told him the chances of them being forced to leave before it was all over were possible. Whether the fire would continue all the way to them, only time would tell. Many factors would influence the outcome. Number one was fuel. Was there enough to feed the fire the three miles of private landscape between where it was burning and the spot he was standing.

The second factor was wind. At the moment it was a light breeze, which could change at any time. Both direction and intensity. If it picked up enough, it wouldn't be very long before the fire was on top of them. And finally, would those brave individuals fighting the blaze get it under control. As dry as it was, he saw little chance of it.

As he waited and watched at first, he thought about putting on some old clothes and going over to the fire to help. The thought didn't last long. There was no room for a man his age and condition there. He'd only get in the way with his brittle bones and stiff, aching muscles. Any of the volunteers, fighting alongside professionals, could do a lot more good toward putting out the fire than he could. The best help he could possibly be, was to stay out of the way.

Dave turned to go back in the house, only to discover that Elaine and Jill were now outside. After getting her dressed, Elaine had wasted no time moving Jill onto her wheelchair and bringing her out to see what was going on. Both were ignoring him and watching the fire. Elaine's face was filled with rapt attention. Jill's was more confused than concerned, but not upset the way she was when she first smelled the smoke.

Concerned or not, when she caught his eye, she gave Dave a big smile anyway. Something he aways got from her every morning, the first time they made eye contact. It was good that she could still smile. There wasn't much else she could do. What was happening to her should never happen to anyone. It was a hard, long time way to die.

When Dave lost his wife, Linda, he thought he would never again feel a pain so great, a loss so deep. She was murdered, so it was as sudden as it was devastating. The moment he was told what happened was locked so tight in his memory that he'd never get rid of it. Every day of his life, he would one way or the other be reminded of that moment. It was always a living hell.

Yet, he often got the feeling that what was happening to Jill was worse. With Linda it was only an instant. She was alive and part of his life, then she was gone, with no chance to return. They never said goodbye. Something no one ever wants to face.

It's better to have that chance. Isn't it? Not always. For more than a year, he and Elaine had been saying goodbye to Jill. Each in their own silent way. Each day, it seemed, they lost another part of her. Some days, life was filled with the heart wrenching feelings of watching someone die a little.

As his head moved from watching Jill to the fire, he felt the tremors of death and dying flow through him. She always seemed delicate, when compared to her sister, Elaine. Elaine, the oldest of the two, was the one who could easily work twelve-hour days tending crops in the field, the always huge garden, and a multitude of animals. She canned, froze, and otherwise processed at least ninety percent of her food, her entire adult life. For the past few years, it'd been a cooperative effort, with the three of them living together.

Up until she started going downhill with what the doctors thought was Parkinson's disease, Jill always assisted in the effort. Now, she needed help in getting in or out of bed, eating, or using toilet. And worst of all, whatever it was that was the cause of her physical problems, was affecting her brain. She had dementia. He didn't believe there was any worse affliction a person could have. Compared to that, cancer is probably kind. It's for sure, never any worse. Parkinson's was not something anyone would want. It would make everything a person did more difficult to do. But the dementia was a living hell to have, to see, to live with.

Dave hated watching it happen to Jill. She was always so kind, so gentle, so all around good. It made no sense that she was the one of them to suffer. He felt he was far more deserving of what she was suffering from than she was. It seemed as if it was always the best who pay the most, and that life was incredibly unfair.

He turned back to face the flames, towering so high, and burning with such intensity that he could've sworn he could feel the heat, even though it was still too far away.

Watching what was happening to the refuge, he had many of the same feelings he had when he thought about Jill. It appeared to be dying quickly, but in truth it'd been dying a relatively slow death for several years. A death he'd been watching closely since it began. A whole community of lifeforms meeting a slow, but constant kind of dying.

It was a relatively new wildlife refuge, as those things go. It was created a few years before he and his then wife, Linda, bought their small farm. A few environmentally conscious men somehow managed to convince the federal government to pay the bill. It was a time close enough to WWII and the depression that people still wanted to do some good things. Unlike now where people rarely get past voting Republican and bitching about taxes.

The people who did the actual work, did a superb job of creating the refuge, a place where all the wildlife, especially the waterfowl, thrived. As all too often happens to good things, especially good things connected to the environment, it quickly changed.

During a time when the Republicans controlled congress and the presidency, a deal was made to sell a large portion of the refuge to a private corporation. They used that part of the refuge, along with a large amount of private land, to build a huge resort/condo/townhouse project. It proved to be immensely profitable most of the time. And even though it suffered its share of disasters, it continued to grow until recently. That was brought to end with new management of the corporation.

The Republican's plan had always been to sell the refuge off completely, so when the corporation announced it wasn't going to buy any more of it, it was put up to be sold to the highest bidder.

A group of environmentally minded citizens, along with the Nature Conservancy, managed to buy it. Much to the chagrin of the Republicans. They didn't want it preserved. An industrial park was closer to what they had in mind. In their way of thinking, anything not making money for some rich person who didn't need more money, was a waste.

They'd been so careful when they wrote the law to ensure that no liberal could ever force cancelation of the sale, they found it impossible to do so when they tried to cancel the sale to environmentalists. And they did try mightily. They were thoroughly incensed to discover that the refuge was now in the hands of a group of people who intended on keeping it a wildlife refuge. All be it one with somewhat more public access than normal for a wildlife refuge.

Watching it burn, Dave temporarily wondered if it was all for naught. Would the fact it burned discourage enough of the people involved in saving it to give up on it, and force it to be sold again? And if it was sold again, would it be turned into an industrial park or some such thing that the rich could profit from?

Unlike Jill, who was never going to get better and return to even part of what she once was, the refuge could and would recover. No matter what a Republican Senator said about the fire burning so hot nothing would grow there for a hundred years.

"It doesn't look good, does it," he said to Elaine.

"No, it doesn't. I'd guess that most of the refuge has already burned, and the rest probably will."

"It'll be a long time recovering from this," he predicted.

Then she did something that momentarily seemed strange. She smiled. "Not anywhere near as long as people might think. I know this is a bad one, but fire is still a part of nature. It'll recover, and the recovery will be quicker than any of the so-called experts on TV or in the government are going to be claiming."

Dave knew she was right. It would recover. Life with Jill, with caring for someone he knew would never recover, made him forget that recovery was possible. Especially something as alive, as vibrant, as was the wildlife refuge. Burned or not, it was still a living, breathing thing. Fire set it back, but it didn't kill it. Only the humans would or could do that.

At the moment though, it seemed as if there wasn't much alive there, other than the fires raging through it. He knew better. Most of the animals would escape the fire itself. Many would likely die later from other causes. Starvation and lack of habitat were the most prevalent reasons.

Soon, his head was filled with all the things that were going to go wrong after the fire was out. At one time, before the invasion of the white man, animals could move on after a fire, if only for a short term. Nowadays there was no place to move on to. The wilderness was pretty much gone. Worldwide. Not just here. So, the fire which in nature could often be a good thing, was now devastating. But as bad as it seemed to him emotionally, he was intelligent enough to know that the refuge, and the life it held, would recover. It would probably take more time than he had left in his life, but given the chance, it would definitely return to what it was before the fire.

Dave was so lost in his thoughts of life in the past and the refuge's future, that he didn't hear the car come up the driveway. The man driving it was out of the car and slammed his door before he noticed him. The man had a big frown on his face when Dave did.

"What's the matter with you people?" he asked as he joined them. "Don't you realize there's an evacuation order out? You're not supposed to be here. I suggest you get moving right now. It's especially important, since you have someone like her here." He pointed at Jill, shaking his hand in her direction.

"Sorry," Dave said. "We didn't know about any order."

"You do now, so you'd best get a move on."

"We will," he told him, "as soon as we get dressed and a few things packed to take along. After, of course, it looks like we need to. Right now, it doesn't."

"I don't think that's what's going to happen. You'll be getting into your vehicle and leaving now!"

That was enough for Dave. He'd tried to be patient with the man. However, the man had already managed to eliminate what little of it Dave had to start with.

"I don't know who you are. I don't know who you think you are. I don't much care either. I know who you aren't. You are definitely not someone who can come here and start ordering us around."

"Actually, I am. I am Jason Johnson, and I am part of Minnesota's new task force. We've been created to assist people at times like this, when their lives might be in danger. We were also commissioned to protect our seniors. Something that obviously needs doing here. Given your callous disregard for that woman's safety in this emergency, I can only imagine the mistreatment she receives from you on a daily basis."

Elaine was only half listening to the man when he first opened his mouth, but he now had her attention. "Like Dave," she said, making no attempt to hide her irritation, "I don't know, nor do I care, who you are. Contrary to what you've said or might say, we are in exactly no immediate danger. If the fire gets this far, it will be quite a while before it does. It will only take us a couple of minutes to be out of here. The roads are good and there's no traffic, nor will there be any. So, we will be leaving if and when it's necessary. Not until."

"And I say you're leaving now. Or else I'll have you arrested."

She attempted a laugh, but it came out more as a snort. "I personally think that you have some ulterior motive for trying to get us to leave. What is it you really want, Jason Johnson? You plan on robbing us blind once we're gone?"

"I have no such intention."

"Then why are you pushing so hard to get us out of here? If you've got something better than what you've been mouthing so far, I want to hear it. Otherwise, get the hell out of here."

"I will not. There was an order given and you must follow it. Everyone must follow orders when they are given. We are a nation of laws, rules and orders, and all must be followed. Therefore, you must leave now, or I will be forced to call the police."

"Go ahead," Elaine answered. "We're going nowhere until if and when it's necessary."

"That's it. You will be arrested. Some time in a jail cell will be good for all three of you."

"So, you're going to have Jill locked up too. What's your reason for that?"

"Simple. She's going along with you, and not cooperating. She's not following my orders. Orders really need to be obeyed."

"So far as we know," Elaine said, making no attempt to hide her contempt for him, "you don't have any right to give us orders. We haven't seen any ID of any kind."

"I'm not required to show ID. I'm part of the task force. We're above that sort of thing."

Dave looked at Elaine. "This guy's an idiot. Should I tell him again to leave, or should I throw his sorry ass out of here?"

"Just forget him. He isn't worth the effort it'd take to throw him out."

"You're right, and he's too stupid to know he should leave."

So, they left him standing there as they watched the fire for a while longer. He was still there when they went back inside to get ready for the day. It was Elaine's week to assist Jill with all her morning preparations, so Dave made breakfast.

He thought the idiot standing out in their yard might be hungry, so he opened the kitchen window. He wanted to make him suffer some. He put together pot of coffee in their old fashioned percolator, as much to create the aroma of brewing coffee as anything. He wasn't sure if it would, but he hoped it would drift out the window far enough to reach the man. Next, he started frying some old-time, smoked in a smokehouse bacon in a cast iron frying pan. The aroma drifting out of the pan was definitely strong enough to reach him.

The farm raised eggs and toast from home baked bread didn't carry near as much of the delicious breakfast smells, but he hoped they would blend with the others enough to surround him. If it did, it would be enough to drive him to distraction.

It did, to some extent. Dave's frequent glances outside as he cooked, verified the fact that Jason definitely was watching the kitchen window. He continued to do so, even after they finished eating and cleaned up the kitchen.

With that done, Dave went back out to check the fire.

It had diminished enough so there was virtually no chance they were in any danger from it. That didn't seem to matter to Jason Johnson, who claimed to be part of a special task force, who was now standing in the yard, waiting for the police to come and arrest them for not evacuating.

CHAPTER 2

Deputy Sheriff Mack Thomas was the kind of friend everyone wants, and sometimes needs. This was a time Dave was grateful for both kinds. Their friendship didn't go back even to Mack's childhood, let alone his own. It started when Mack first returned home after a few years riding rodeo. He rode bulls mostly, but was known to take on horses too, both saddle and bareback broncs.

It was after his father, Ben Thomas, had an auction of antiques he hadn't previously realized he owned, which was so successful it made him near rich. He had hired Dave and his brother Paul to do some much needed repairs around his farm.

As time went on, they did ever more work for all of the Thomas family, and became good friends with all of them. Mack especially, even after he made some kind of connection with Dave's wife, Linda. No one could figure out what, exactly, that connection was. Not even they could. But there was something special, something somehow pure about it, so that it was accepted by everyone. Even Lisa, who was now Mack's wife.

Growing out of that relationship, was a special kind of friendship Lisa and Dave had. They'd come close a couple of times to bringing it into that other dimension, but wisely came to the mutual decision it would be best not to.

Mack knew of, and approved, that friendship. Even though what they had between them wasn't the same as a lifelong friendship, what they did have was as strong.

So, it was good for Dave to see him, and from his simple greeting of a nod of his head and a slight smile, he could tell Mack was equally glad to see them. They knew that because it was a day that would take a lot to make Mack smile. Even the small one he gave them. No one loved the refuge more that he did, so the loss from the fire was devastating for him.

But being the man he was, he overcame it and immediately asked the man in their driveway, trying to get Mack's attention, what the problem was.

"I demand you arrest these people," the man said, drooling slightly in his excitement.

The look Mack gave him before he answered wasn't exactly friendly. "What for?"

"They refused to evacuate when ordered to, and they are obviously abusing that poor woman in the wheelchair."

"It doesn't appear to me that there was any need to evacuate. And these people are not now and never have abused anyone."

"They most certainly have. They had her out in the yard while the fire was burning, and refused to evacuate when so ordered."

"Who gave the order?"

"Well, I did, of course."

"So...who in the hell are you?"

"I am a member of the state's special task force created to protect all citizens, especially the elderly, in times of need. We are authorized to act in situations like this, to ensure that the type of behavior these people have demonstrated is not tolerated. They have broken the law, so I demand you arrest them. I want the two of them in jail, and that poor abused soul in the wheelchair placed in a home where she will be safe and secure."

"Well, Mister Task Force, do you have some ID to show me?"

"As a member of the task force, I am not required to carry any special identification. And you, as a member of law enforcement, are required to follow my instructions."

It took an effort for Mack to not verbally rip the man's head off. "I don't know what world you came from," he told the man, "but not this one, we don't arrest people on the word of a stranger with no ID."

"But you have too. It is the Law."

"No, I most certainly don't have to. So, I think it's past time for you to get the hell out of here and leave these good people alone."

"You can't tell me what to do. I'm a member of the task force. Only my manager can tell me what to do."

"So, who's your manager? Who do you work for?"

"My manager is Dell Whitcomb. I work for the Heavenly Homes Corporation."

"Those bastards! It's not hard to see what you're up to. I suggest you get the hell off this property and out of here. You've got two minutes and if you're not gone, I'm arresting you for trespassing."

"You can't..."

"You've got one minute." Mack took out his handcuffs.

The man left.

Dave was shaking his head during their entire conversation. All he could say to Mack when the guy left was, "Thanks. He was a real pest."

"He was that, but don't thank me yet. That Heavenly Homes corporation he works for has bought up a large portion of the nursing homes in Minnesota. And all over the country, actually. One way or the other, they've been forcing people into those homes."

What Mack told him triggered the memory of something he'd learned fairly recently. "From what I've read, Mack, this kind of thing is already going on in about twenty-five states. And it's expected to spread farther. The corporations doing it have grown fast since the Republicans allowed Medicare to pay a much higher amount for people staying in nursing homes."

"Yes, another big-time corporate scam, once again endorsed by the Republicans. Heavenly Homes is a big enough corporation now to buy off all the politicians they need to get the kind of legislation passed to make a lot of what they do legal. That task force the guy threatened you with is just one piece of the bullshit."

Before Dave could say more, Mack's cell phone went off. He answered it, and listened for a few moments after his initial hello. When he did speak, there was little doubt in his mind what the call was about.

"No, Dale, I will not call and apologize to anyone connected to that company for any reason. Not now, not ever. What they're doing is what's wrong. It's criminal. And please, be the friend you've always been, and never ask me, or even suggest to me, to do that again." He hung up the phone.

"I hope we didn't get you in any trouble, Mack," Dave said.

"No, not at all. That was just Dale, being the Sheriff. He knows what an exercise in futility it is to ask me to kowtow to people who work for a corporation like that one. But sometimes he does what he believes he should do, even if he doesn't like it any more than I do."

"I appreciate that. One of the world's biggest problems is the fact people too easily back down from those in power."

"They do. If it weren't for people like you, who are willing to stand up for their own rights in spite of a lot of power against them, I think I'd have lost all faith in humanity a long time ago."

"It would be easy to do. Especially in your line of work. For me, I don't know if, at my age, I'd have the courage to do much at all without friends like you."

"I think you have it, Dave. Since I've known you, you've always shown an extraordinary amount of courage. And I don't mean to bring up past, painful things, but I have to say, I've never seen a braver man than you were when we lost Linda."

"You held up pretty well yourself, Mack. I know how you felt about her. You even managed to hold back the tears."

"No, I didn't. I just didn't cry when I was supposed to."

"Either way, we lost a lot when we lost her. And of all the things she was, and she was so many wonderful things, I think I miss the simple friendship we had as much as anything. And as you know, with Linda close, there was a lot of love and living. I knew I could always count on her if I ever needed her."

Suddenly the memory of so many friends overwhelmed Dave. He guessed it was a day for memories. He wasn't sure if it was the fire or the idiot who visited to threaten them that caused them to start, but they were there. They stood, silent, both of them filled with things remembered. For Dave, it was Linda first. Then they drifted back in time. One that flashed through his head was when he met Elaine and Jill. It was in the middle of a blizzard, way back when he was married to his second wife. He found Jill on the side of a highway in the raging storm. They knew they couldn't get far, so they tried for her sister's, which was a small farm. Elaine was the sister. The refuge from the storm turned into several memorable days. It might have ended there, but fate decided otherwise. And now, at the end of their lives, they were living together as their own kind of family. The kind of family the Heavenly Homes Corporation would be more than happy to destroy.

CHAPTER 3

A couple of days following the fire, Mack and Lisa Thomas started the day the same way they did as often as they could. Eating breakfast with his family. The conversation started and stayed rather lively. Two topics were on their minds.

The refuge fire was foremost, but not too far behind was a concern about Dave Thomas and the corporation determined to force his live-in, Jill, into their nursing home. A place, they all knew, that was no more than a half step from a living hell.

Mack's uncle Roy asked the question on everyone's mind. "What do you think's going to happen with the refuge, now that most of it has burned?"

"It'll come back. It looks like hell right now, but fire is part of nature's cycle. Even the bad ones like we had. They're normally rare, but part of the cycle."

"It's sad though, to see it the way it is now."

"Yes, but it could be a lot worse. Bull dozers trashing it to fulfill some rich man's wet dream would be worse."

Roy laughed. "You sure don't care much for the rich folk, do you, Mack?"

"For the most part no, I don't. I can't see much reason to have any fondness for those who spend their lives trying to get more when they've already got way more than what they can ever use, let alone need."

"Be hard for me to argue with you on that point. A person's got to wonder where greed that strong comes from."

"I don't know that I care, Roy. Where it comes from, why it exists, will never make it right. What they've always wanted to do to the refuge was and is wrong. What's downright evil, is what that Heavenly Homes Corporation is trying to do to Dave Sanders and his two live-ins, Jill and Elaine."

"I heard about that," Roy said. "Forcing people into those so-called nursing homes is about as lowlife as it gets."

"It is. And the sole purpose for doing it is to make some already rich people that much richer."

"It's too bad, Mack, that there's nothing we can do about it."

"I know. Who knows though? Someone might come up with something."

"I guess it's possible someone might." Roy gave Mack a half smile. "Yes, you never know what someone might come up with."

Mack knew Roy had some kind of idea, but before he could question him, his cell phone rang. He knew from the ring that it was sheriff Dale Magee calling. "What's up?" he answered.

"I'm at the refuge, Mack. The fire people have found the source of the fire. They know where and why it started."

"What started it?"

"That's why I'm calling you. It involves a homicide. I've already called Paul," he said, referring to the sheriff department's detective, Paul Danielson. "I think it'd be a good idea for you to check it out too."

"How quick do you need me there?"

"Not a huge rush, Mack. But the sooner you get here, the sooner we can finish the investigation here."

"Okay, Dale. I'll be there shortly." Mack decided to leave right away. His curiosity about what caused the fire was stronger than the hunger pangs in his stomach.

"What is it, Mack?" his wife Lisa asked as he got up to leave.

"They found the cause of the fire. It has something to do with a homicide, so Dale wants me to come and take a look."

"He misses too many more meals," his father, Ben, said as Mack left. "And he's gonna waste away."

"Yeah," Roy's wife, Wanda said, "but that's Mack. Duty calls, he goes."

"Don't you guys be picking on him," Lisa said. "He just tries to do what he thinks is right."

"We'd be the last to fault him for being who he is," Roy explained. "It's just that he always puts everyone else first. That can get a body to worrying about him some. It seems, sometimes, that he ought to take some better care of himself."

"I'm working on that," she told them.

Ben changed the subject with a question for Roy. "You smiled, Roy, when you told Mack that someone might come up with something pertaining to those nursing homes. I know from the look that you've got something cooking in that devious brain of yours. So, what the hell is it?"

"Nothing definite. I'm only kicking around some ideas on how to get inside one of those places, and maybe see how they operate. Possibly do it from the receiving end of their so-called care."

"That might not be such a good idea. It could get dangerous."

"That's part of what's egging him on," Wanda said. "He's been antsy for a while and needs something to stimulate him. So don't be surprised."

"All you Thomas men have that in you," Theresa, Ben's wife said. "It seems like, sooner or later, you got to do something radical. Even Ben, settled as he is, has some of that in him. But you, Roy, are the worst. Wanda's a real saint sometimes, for putting up with you."

Roy laughed. "You're right," he agreed. "Thing is though, the sainthood stuff goes both ways. Wanda's been known to have her days too."

"There isn't any of us that should be pointing fingers," Wanda told them. "Look at Lisa here. She's the youngest of us. She's a short timer as far as being part of this family is concerned. Yet she's had more than her share of adventure since she joined us and then became a sheriff's deputy."

"You're right, Wanda," Ben said. "We're all guilty. Even Theresa, who actually tries hard to avoid trouble, finds her share of it. But she's right about one thing. None of us actually looks for some kind of action the way Roy does. So, tell us Roy, what is it that you're cooking up this time?"

"Nothing all that serious. Just like maybe getting myself put into one of those places. So I can watch and see how and what they do. Be nice to catch them doing things we could hang their ass for."

"It would be nice," Lisa agreed. "But before you do anything like that, I think it'd be a good idea to talk it over with Mack."

"I suppose, but I can take care of myself you know."

Lisa shook her head yes. "Of course you can. Probably better than any of us. Mack included. But if you do it, it would still be a good idea to have some sort of backup plan. And that's something Mack can best help with."

"I don't have any intention of doing anything right now," Roy told her. "So, there'll be plenty of time for Mack and I to go over my ideas before I do."

"Good. But now it's time for me to go to work. There's lots of crime out there to be stopped." She laughed, as if her comment were a joke.

They all knew it wasn't. Lisa and Mack were two people guilty of doing their jobs too well. That meant they were in frequent danger.

So, the four people left behind, sitting at the breakfast table, worried incessantly about them. None of the four would ever consider telling them they shouldn't do their jobs. But that didn't mean they didn't want them to ease up some.

CHAPTER 4

Mack drove deep into the burned out refuge before he reached the place the fire started. Several people were already there. The two he was looking for were off to the side, talking with a man he didn't know.

"Morning, Dale, morning, Paul," he said as he walked up to them.

They returned his greeting, then Dale said, "Mack, this is Jonas Wagner. He's the fire investigator who found this location."

Mack shook his hand. "What caused the fire?" he asked, without any preliminaries.

Jonas gave Mack an exasperated look. "If you bothered to look, I wouldn't have to tell you," he complained.

Mack was feeling every bit as impatient and frustrated as he was. He shook his head, and moved closer to the spot the man was pointing at. It was thoroughly charred body, of which there wasn't enough left to be sure of anything about it.

"Someone tried to get rid of it by burning it. Whoever it was, probably used a can of gasoline. It was about a as stupid a thing they could have done, dry as it is."

"For sure," Mack answered. "There's little doubt about it, this was a murder. Given the condition of the body, it's not going to tell us much. But at least we know what caused the fire." He looked at Jonas with a new respect. "You must have put in a lot of time to find this, given how far into the refuge it is."

Jonas shook his head. "Not as much as you might think. Every fire has a story to tell. If you know how to follow the evidence it leaves behind, you can usually find the cause. I didn't have to walk all of it to find this one."

Mack told him. "That's still really doing good work." He turned to Dale and Paul. "Do you two have any ideas?" he asked them.

"Just one," Paul said. "A young lady went missing the night the fire started. Her name was Mattie Jared. She was taken at that station on the highway..." He went on to tell Mack what he knew about her disappearance, then finished with, "She was taken late, somewhere between eleven and midnight. The station attendant didn't notice that her car was still parked at the station until after two AM. It was a slow night so he remembered her."

"Is he the one who reported her missing?"

"No, her parents did. They went looking for her when she didn't return home. They knew she was going to stop at the station, so they went there first. They called our office from there."

"Do you think it'll be possible to ID her?"

"It should be. Dental records if there are any. And there should be enough of her left to check her DNA. If it's the young lady we think it is, we should be able to ID her that way."

"This sure isn't anything we needed right now, is it, Paul?"

"It isn't. But when is it, Mack?"

"I know. Never. I sure wouldn't mind going back to the days when the refuge was still whole and the worst crime we had in the county was teenage drunk driving."

"Was it really that much better?"

"Actually, yes, it was. But now, so many of the problems aren't just caused by that miserably resort. A whole lot of them are national and are a direct result of national politics and problems."

"I couldn't agree more. But we can't stop fighting back every way we can. We do, and it'll all be over."

"You don't have to remind me. So, who's going to be the primary on this investigation?"

"I think I should take it. I think it'll be a good case to begin Lisa's detective training, and you've got plenty of other things to deal with. Also, the one that needs most looking into, you're more informed about than I am."

"You referring to Dave Sander's problem?"

"I am. What's going on there is one of the dirtiest scams I've ever seen. Forcing people into nursing homes. Death camps is a better term. So don't hesitate to ask, if there's ever anything I can do to help."

"That goes both ways, Paul."

Dale finally interrupted them. "Don't I have anything to say about what my deputies work on?"

Mack and Paul both smiled. "Of course you do," Paul answered. "But you're such a good boss, that you usually let Mack and me figure these things out."

"I'll second that one," Mack added.

This time Dale smiled. "And you're both full of shit. But go ahead. I'd argue with you if I saw the need, but I don't see one here."

"That's because you're the good boss we said you were."

"Okay, that's enough bullshit for one day."

Jonas, who'd been watching them through the whole conversation, asked Dale. "Is that the way they always talk to you?"

"Often enough to remind me who I really am."

"And who's that?"

"A lucky man. To have men like those two on my side is pure luck."

"Don't you feel sometimes, like they're undermining your authority?"

"Not at all. If you knew how many times those two have made me look good, you'd never have to ask that question."

Mack interrupted. "Don't let him kid you, Jonas. The real reason he looks good is because he is good. And one of the ways he's exceptional, is his knack for knowing when to let loose of us enough so we can do our jobs the way we're supposed to. Damn few bosses, be they a sheriff or anything else, are either smart enough or big enough to do that."

"I see how it works for all of you now," Jonas said. "There's been plenty of days when I'd have given a lot to have our department run the way yours does."

That ended their conversation. Since Paul was going to handle that investigation, Mack felt free to leave.

His first stop was a visit with Dave Sanders, to see if there'd been any more harassment from the man who claimed to be a member of the special task force.

"Not since you ran him off," Dave answered when asked. "I'm hoping he learned something from you, and will stay the hell away."

"I'm hoping the same thing, but we shouldn't count on it. Those kind of people aren't likely to quit. They're too filled with greed. Either that, or stupid enough to follow some real bad orders. In the case of that one, I'd say stupid wins."

"You're right. They have to be one or the other, to be cruel enough to force people into those places. You'd think, given the real dedication of most of the people who are the care givers there, that they'd be decent places to live. It doesn't seem though, that anyone's quite figured out how to do that yet."

"I think a large part of it, Dave, is because we all too often don't know how to treat each other as individuals. Especially not within, or dealing with, institutions. No matter who, what, where, or why, rules is rules. Being flexible would make too much sense."

"I think you're right, Mack. I spent a lot of my working life fighting that way of doing things. Not that it did much good. I found life better working with my brother. Just the two of us could often get a hell of a lot more done than all too many groups do now."

"And that's why I far prefer to be on my own every day. It might be safer with two riding together, but it's easier to breathe when you're on your own."

"I probably shouldn't ask this, but I'm going to anyway. Do you feel the same way about your wife being out there alone?"

"Hell no. It scares me. That said, she's out there alone most days, and I don't complain about it. She prefers to ride solo most of the time. I don't believe I have the right to tell her she can't. That goes for most of what she does."

"Good for you, Mack. That's the way it should be."

"It is. I think I can thank you and Linda for teaching me how important it is to give your partner enough space to be whatever it is they should be. Lisa and I would probably do okay even if I treated her like a normal husband would. Thing is, we get along a lot better this way."

Before anymore was said, a car pulled into the driveway. Four men got out. Among them was the man who claimed to be a member of the new special task force. A group set up by a Republican dominated state government. It was organized primarily to force people into now highly profitable nursing homes. He didn't appear to be in charge of the group however, one of the other men was in front of the group as they approached Dave and Mack.

"Which one of you is Dave Sanders?" he asked.

"Before we answer that," Mack told him. "Who do you think you are?"

"I'm Dell Whitcomb," he said, trying to sound macho. "Manager from Heavenly Homes. I have court order to pick up the lady here, who is under extreme duress from the constant mistreatment she's been getting."

"Ain't no damn body here who fits that description, so I suggest you turn your ass around and hike it out of here."

"We will do no such thing. We will use force, if needed, to deliver that poor woman to the safety of our facility."

"Not hardly. There's no way you're going to pull that crap here."

"Yes, we certainly will. As you can see, there are four of us. I can only see two of you. You cannot possible stop us."

Mack peeled back the light jacket he was wearing. "As you can see," he said, "I am a deputy sheriff. I am also armed. You try to kidnap anyone here, and I will be forced to shoot you." He looked at the other three men. "That includes you too," he told them.

Even though two of the men were well over six feet and heavily muscled, they went back to the car they came in. "Hey, you two," Dell Whitcomb yelled, "get back here."

They stood quietly, shaking their heads no.

"You got your answer," Mack told him. "Now get off this property."

"You can't do this," Dell complained. "I have a court order."

"Maybe you do, maybe you don't. Either way, if you don't get moving right now, what you're going to have the most of, is sore wrists from the cuffs I'm going to put on you when I arrest you."

"You can't arrest me. I have a court order."

"Truth is, I can. You're guilty of trespassing, home invasion, and attempted kidnapping. So, one last time, get out of here."

"I will not. You don't have the authority to arrest me."

"Actually, I do." Mack turned him around and slapped the cuffs on him. "You three," he said to the others, "best haul yourselves out of here. If not, I'll be arresting the lot of you as soon as I have this one loaded in my pickup."

They were gone before Mack had Dell loaded.

He turned back to Dave. "I won't be able to make the charges stick," he said, "but it won't hurt for you to come in and press charges. The more difficult we can make it for him the better."

"I'll be in right behind you," Dave agreed.

He went in to tell Elaine, who'd been watching to proceedings out the window, what was happening and where he was going.

"That's good," she said. "But I'd appreciate it if you'd come right back. I think I'm getting the flu or something, so it'll be better if you're the one who takes care of Jill the rest of the day."

"If you're not feeling up to it now, I can skip going into town."

"No, you really should go. Just come back when you're done."

"Okay, I'll get back as soon as I can."

He did, but Elaine was in bed when he got back. It wasn't at all like her to get sick or go the bed so early in the day even if she was, but he tried to keep from worrying about it.

All his plans for the day were for work that needed doing outside, but because of his concern about Elaine, he stayed inside. Jill's needs took up much of his time. He helped her on and off the commode several times. Cooked her a light lunch, then supper. He sat with her and fed her both meals. They normally gave her a bath everyday, but she forgot to tell him of her needs one time. After he removed her diaper, he cleaned her the best he could, then took her into the bathroom for a sponge bath. He gave her a chocolate ice cream sandwich for a treat in the evening. By the time she finished it, she was only a half-step from needing another bath. At bedtime he changed her from her day clothes to her pajamas. By the time she was tucked safely in bed, he was exhausted. He was also hoping Elaine would be feeling better in the morning. Being a lone 24/7 caregiver seemed at least three times as hard as it was with two of them doing it.

When Elaine left the bed the next morning, she didn't look all that great. She improved some after a long shower and a good hair combing. By afternoon she was presentable, even if she felt anything but.

CHAPTER 5

The four men sat at a table near the back of the bar. It was the kind of spot they liked, secluded. Given the topic of their conversation, they knew it was best if they weren't overheard.

"We've got the sure deal," Devon Kost, the biggest man at the table, told the man sitting across from them. "We take them at 24/7 service stations. Lots of them don't even stop for gas, they just go inside for groceries and stuff. We even took one right here, just outside Kingsburg. The other's was from outstate. You should come with us some night. We'll share her, before we finish her."

"What did you do with the body of the one you took here?" the man across from Devon asked.

"Well, that didn't turn out quite like we expected."

"You guys were the ones who started the fire, weren't you?"

"Well, yeah, but we won't do that again."

"I would hope not. Burning down that refuge got a lot more people interested in what you did than just the murder and rape would have."

"Like I said," Devon complained to the man, "We won't be doing anything like that again."

"That's good, because I sure wouldn't want to be part of a fiasco like that was."

"You gonna ride with us then?"

"I'm not sure, but if I do, you're going to have to turn the woman over to me when you're done with her."

"I don't know about that," Devon argued. "The killin' part is almost as good as takin' them. Not to mention having them."

"Well, that's the way it's got to be if I'm to be part of this."

Devon and his two friends weren't sure they liked the idea, but went along with it anyway. They had no trouble grabbing another girl but had a large disagreement with the man when he insisted on being the first to rape her. Again, they didn't like it, but let him do it to her first.

When he finished, he pulled a small pistol from a holster on his ankle and told them, "I kind of hate doing this with you guys, but I have to take this young lady with me. And I'll need to use your van to do it. He told them where he'd leave it, then left with the tied-up girl.

It was a discouraged three men who walked home that night. It was a jubilant man who drove his victim to a very old, long ago abandoned, farmstead. He took her inside the farmhouse, and there he forced her into a large dog kennel. One of several in the room. All but one of the others were occupied by an almost nude young woman.

It was the kind of operation the three men would never have been capable organizing. They couldn't get beyond the idea of grab, rape, and murder. Which is what they continued to do.

The man, on the other hand, notified the people he worked with, that he had enough bodies in stock to fill their order.

Satisfied that he had things under control, he enjoyed a few drinks with the men who he shared his lucrative business with. A business they had every intention of expanding.

CHAPTER 6

Lisa was very grateful for the chance to work with Paul when he told her about it. Even more, she was excited about it. It meant she'd be riding with him as long as she worked this case with him. As much as she liked riding solo, this opportunity was worth more than that was. And with Paul, she'd have none of the problems she'd had riding with some of the male deputies in the past. Especially the younger ones.

He was a lot older than she was, and always treated her with the utmost respect. He was also happily married and had no interest in pursuing any kind of improper relationship.

And best of all, Mack not only approved of her accepting the assignment, he was almost as excited about it as she was. What she didn't expect, was that she would be at a new crime scene after just over an hour of her first day riding with Paul.

They'd barely left the office when they got the call. The body of the girl, who they found out was only seventeen after she was identified, was found in a ditch. It was along a narrow backroad, a few miles north of the burned-out refuge.

It was a horrible thing to look at. It appeared as though she'd been mutilated in nearly every way possible. Lisa immediately studied the ground around the crime scene, all the time taking photos. Next, she knelt next to the body, examining the damage and taking more photos.

When she finished, she told Paul, "I think there were three of them. One was bigger than the other two. I'm pretty sure he raped her first. One of the others was up close to watch. Down on his hands and knees, actually. His nose close to the rape itself. The third watched from a distance, but enjoyed what he saw. There are still traces of semen where he stood. We've got some real sickos to deal with again."

"I have to agree with you, Lisa," Paul said. "And I have to tell you, for someone relatively new to all this, that's a real good evaluation of the scene. No, it's actually a good one even for an experienced detective."

"This is something I think I hope to be able to do a decent job of. I've been doing some heavy reading, and the art of crime scene evaluation is covered in a lot of books and articles. I just hope I can be of some help when it comes to actually catching the men guilty of this."

"I'm sure you will be," Paul said, doing his best to sound encouraging. "There's still a lot for you to learn, but with your intelligence and natural instincts, I can't see anyway you won't be an asset."

She relished his praise, but at the same time knew they were likely to have a big disagreement in the near future. She also expected the same argument with Dale and Mack. After the crime scene visit, she, along with everyone else, knew the three men must be caught soon. Nothing else would stop their killing. She also knew how difficult it was to track down and catch people guilty of this kind of random killing.

The problem she was facing, was convincing everyone that the plan she was beginning to develop in her head was feasible. She had no doubts about the reaction she was going to get when she presented it. She also knew she had to be prepared if she was going to get them to so much as listen to it. For them to accept it, it would have to be near perfect. For that to happen, she began her preparations.

To start, the latest victim, who like the first was taken from the parking lot of a 24/7 service station, was wearing a skirt, which in their haste to hurt her, they didn't bother to remove. They also left her socks and shoes on. Her hands were also tied behind her, using plastic zip ties. All points Lisa could use.

The heart of her plan, and what all of them would object to, was using herself as a decoy to trap the three men. They would consider that as putting herself in way too much danger. She didn't think so. Once she had the details worked out, she was sure she could pull it off without putting herself into much danger at all.

To start with, she would wear a pair of bulky socks. Bulky enough to hide a derringer at her ankle. She just needed to find the right holster to hold it there fairly tight, yet still allow her to pull it loose quickly.

She also intended to have another defensive weapon. Since deciding to go into law enforcement, she'd constantly read about all aspects of it. Weapons is one of the subjects she'd studied the hardest. So, she already had a defensive weapon picked out.

It was a small, very thin, switchblade knife. One with a retractable blade, rather than one that flips out. To start her plan, she purchased four of them. Then, slowly and carefully, she began sharpening them. Her plan was to take them past razor sharp. Surgically sharp was her goal.

With the knives as sharp as she wanted them, she picked out her clothing. The most important article was her skirt. The one she needed and found was a full skirt, solid black one with a wide waist band. To the inside of the waistband, she sewed a wide piece of elastic, by the bottom and side edges only. She had dyed it to match the skirt color.

After practicing a few times, with her hands held behind her as if they were tied, the pocket she'd created with the elastic proved to work exactly as she wanted it to. Now that she had a pocket just right for one of her newly sharpened knives, she spent a few more hours practicing. She always held her hands behind her as if they were tied, to learn how to use the knife properly. It only took a few tries to learn how to remove the knife from its pocket, snap it open, and cut the shadow Zip ties. She continued to do it repeatedly anyway. She wanted all of the motions she took to do it to be second nature. If she had to think about it, it might be too slow.

Sooner than she originally hoped, she was ready to try it for real. She wanted a site similar to the one the killer/rapists would choose. So, she took Mack out into the wooded area behind their house. She was wearing the skirt she'd prepared, with a knife in the waist band. She also brought zip ties. When they reached the right spot, she gave them to Mack.

"Tie my hands behind me," she asked.

"Why?"

"I'd tell you, but it's better I show you. So, please, tie my hands."

"Is this some new sex game?"

"Not now. Maybe later we can work it into one later. No, for now, just do what I ask. It's important."

"I don't know that I like this, but okay." He tied her hands.

"Now lay me down my back and get on top of me. Pull my skirt up to my waist and open your pants like you're going to rape me."

Mack shook his head, showing his distaste for what he was doing. When his pants were open, he looked up to find a knife close to his throat. The knife was in Liza's hand.

She quickly retracted it as he asked, "Where the hell did that come from?"

"My skirt," she explained, then showed him the system she'd worked out with the knives, and the derringer at her ankle.

"That's a pretty neat setup," he said, "but what's it good for?"

"Capturing the three men who've already committed two murders that we know of, and who we know will commit a lot more if we don't stop them. I want to be a decoy. If they grab me, I can subdue them before they do anything to me."

"You don't really believe they'll give up that easy, do you?"

"The way I have it planned, yes I do."

"And how do you have it planned?"

"I will take them out."

"I don't know if I like the sound of that."

"What do you want me to say? I'll be a good little girl and let them go on raping and murdering innocent women? I don't think so. I want them stopped. I want all men who do what they do stopped. And the truth is, it doesn't really matter how I do it. Whatever they get, however they end up, they deserve it."

"That's pretty strong, Lisa."

"It was meant to be, Mack. If you think it's too strong, then you're not the man I thought you were."

"No, it just seems awful strong coming from you."

"Does it? If you were me, would you feel any different?"

"I can't say I would. I'd probably be reacting even stronger. But that doesn't mean I can let you get yourself into a situation that gets you hurt or even killed."

"I don't plan on it. No matter what though, I'll always go after men like those three, and I'll always do what it takes to stop them."

"Even killing them?"

"Or worse, if necessary."

Mack shook his head. He knew more arguing wasn't going to change her mind. The only way to stop her now, would be Dale telling her no. He doubted that would happen. The men needed to be stopped, and Lisa's plan was a good one. There were no legitimate reasons to tell her no, so the only reason Dale might would be to sooth Mack's nerves, and that was very unlikely. Doing it would only be fair to Mack. No one else. So, Mack didn't say anything when Dale okayed Lisa's plan. Especially not when even Paul thought it was a good one.

Before they could move forward with it, however, a third girl was found murdered.

Her body was in the same horrible condition as the first two. Finding the body made it easier on Lisa though. It took most of the negative pressure about her decoy plan off her. Mack was the one who found the body, and that was enough to stop him from trying to convince anyone that there should be another way to stop the murderers.

This murder also helped in a couple of other ways. By following the pattern of where the girls were taken, it gave everyone involved in implementing Lisa's plan a good indication where they might try for the next girl. And given the intelligence level of the killers, it would never occur to them to change the pattern.

The second thing that helped was the time the girls were taken. All three were taken within the same two-hour time frame. And again, there was never any thought to change that either. Not by the three anyway.

Because the murders were coming closer together, it was decided to begin with Lisa's plan the second night after the third girl was found. To act as the decoy, she drove into the service station and parked in front, the same as the three murdered girls. She went inside the station, bought a few things, then left. She did that at four random times for three nights with no results. They were getting somewhat discouraged, but on the second stop the forth night, the three men grabbed Lisa.

They tied her hands behind her with zip ties after throwing her into the back seat of their car. The smallest of the three drove the vehicle, and the other two got in the back with her. They were on either side of her, and began to maul her immediately, something she hadn't anticipated.

She could have gone for her knife right away, but knew her chances were far better if she waited until they were out of the car. They thought they were being real strong men by grabbing her in all the places she'd never want their hands. They weren't. They didn't know Lisa, nor did they have the ability to imagine a woman ever being as capable of defending herself as she was.

They couldn't get beyond their excitement of having taken a woman as beautiful as Lisa was. They were so excited they never even considered going beyond ripping open her blouse and her bra off. The big man, Devon Kost, was so anxious that he took his pants down before he even lifted her skirt.

As soon as he completed that task and grabbed his manhood to wave it at Lisa, she went into action. With her hands now totally free and holding the switchblade, she made one quick slash that cut off his cherished manhood as close to his body as was possible.

He screamed as he jumped away, throwing his hands in the air. The man kneeling close to them made a grab for her knife. She was way too fast for him and swung the knife at him. He was only wearing a light tee-shirt, so her knife easily cut through it and went up to the hilt when she pushed it into his stomach. She left a cut there about eight inches long and nearly two inches deep. He too, jumped back and tried to stop the bleeding, as well as stuff his guts back inside his body.

The third man, standing back away with his manhood held securely in his right hand, was a bit slow going for the gun tucked into his belt. Lisa got to her derringer first. They were close enough to each other so even it was accurate. Her first shot hit him in the chest, just slightly above the heart. It didn't kill him. Her second shot hit his forehead. It did kill him.

With the three murderers subdued, she called her backup with her location, and suggested that they call an ambulance. As she waited, she did nothing to help the wounded men. As far as she was concerned, they were still conscious, so it was up to them to stop their own bleeding. If they couldn't, well, they'd just have to bleed.

As everyone arrived there was the usual confusion and excitement. Lisa calmly answered questions and tried to stay out of the way of those who were actually doing something.

Then she overheard one of the paramedics from the ambulance, who didn't have much of an idea what it was all about say, "We should try to find this man's penis. Maybe it can be reattached."

Lisa knew where it was laying on the ground. It was close, so she casually moved over to it. It only took a slight movement of her foot to bring her heel over the lost penis. She brought it down on it, and as hard as she could, she ground it down. It was a rather tattered piece of flesh when she again moved her foot.

"Attach that," she thought, "if you can."

Both men survived their wounds, but there was no reattachment. And once they were in prison, they were each in their own way a special attraction.

The one with the knife wound in the stomach needed to be fed a special diet, due to the severe damage his guts had suffered. Since prison food left a lot to be desired already, his diet was incredibly bad. So bad, that he quickly lost half his weight.

The big man, Devon Kost, who considered himself super macho, attracted all manner of macho prisoners. His build was now rather unique, and it was checked out on a regular basis. That, and a more rear portion of his anatomy.

CHAPTER 7

The media had been full of the murders since the first one. They loved reporting them, and as they learned how Lisa was the one to capture the guilty men, she was the object of their attention for several days. They especially played up the part of the man losing his penis, and how it was mysteriously mangled after the fact.

A few macho males condemned her for defending herself against him the way she did, claiming there had to be a better way. They were very much in the minority though. Most people thought it was a fitting end to a rapist, and a lot of women were sorry that she didn't do it to all three of the men.

The one thing that was different with this incident, compared to so many other acts of violence by the police, is that no one was screaming for her to be disciplined in any way. Not even the macho males.

The downside of it was the fact that it made Lisa's job as deputy sheriff extremely difficult. If it wasn't the media looking for another interview, it was the general public trying to get her attention. It got so bad for a while that she actually volunteered to help Dale with much of the dreaded paperwork involved in being sheriff.

Working inside as opposed to being out and about afforded her a place to hide from the constant harassment for a while. It also gave her something she never expected to need. A firsthand knowledge of what it takes to run a sheriff's department as large as Clayborne County's had grown to be.

Being the kind of person she was, she put everything she had into the work. She might not like it, but it needed doing, and it gave Dale a much needed break from its drudgery. It also put her in his good graces in a way that nothing else could. Something that would benefit her in the not too distant future. She also learned in a short time, which of the people working in the office were dedicated to it, and who it was that never did any more than the minimum required.

When she finally escaped the office, most of the frenzy over her had died down. Even so, she occasionally had to put up with, one kind or another, of attention or harassment from the public.

The worst were the macho males, all of whom were absolutely sure they could convince her to go out with them. And once there, of course, they'd get her in bed. Lisa would have none of it, and her patience often wore thin.

What helped her get through that more than anything else was her relationship with her husband. Mack understood what she'd been going through, and was always there to support her during those times she was justifiably upset by it.

She also had the full support of hers and Mack's family. But the one person besides Mack who often gave her the most comfort, was her friend Dave Sanders. He somehow always seemed to know the right way to react when she was troubled, no matter what that trouble might be.

Recently, however, she'd been reluctant to bother him with any of her problems. Between taking care of Jill, dealing with constant harassment from the government and the Heavenly Homes people, he had his hands full.

It was getting to the point that he could barely function beyond doing the day to day caregiving Jill needed. He also had to constantly give moral support to Elaine, Jill's sister. She'd always been extremely vigorous and active, taking care of the garden and their many animals. Now, she was slowing down. She wasn't sick, she was simply aging, and with that aging, because of so many years of hard work, her body was showing the toll that hard work took.

What was happening to Dave, Elaine, and Jill was as much cause for concern for Ben and Theresa and Roy and Wanda, as it was for Mack and Lisa. But Lisa was the one who brought it up at breakfast one morning.

"We need to find a way to make it easier for Dave and Elaine to take care of Jill. It's difficult enough, without the constant harassment from those Heavenly Homes people."

"I have an idea on how to help them out," Roy said. "It'll cost us money, but not so much any of us will notice."

"You know we don't give a damn about the money," Mack answered. "So let's hear your ideas."

"We can get those Heavenly Homes people off their backs if they are in an official assisted living arrangement."

"There's no way Dave," Lisa argued, "or even Elaine would go for that. They're determined to stay in their home, and take care of Jill there. And it's only right that they should be able to."

"I agree," Roy said. "What I have in mind will let them do that. That is what's going to cost some money. We can turn their home into an assisted living arrangement. There'll probably need to be some plumbing and other structural changes made. We'll also have to hire a professional staff to run the place."

"I don't know," Mack questioned, "won't the powers that be find some way to block them from starting their own assisted living place?"

"More than likely. But that's where we come in. We should start our own corporation. The corporation can lease their home from them, then make them our first clients."

"Damn, but you have been thinking, Roy. I think it's a great idea."

"It's going to cost a pretty fair amount though. This kind of thing ain't cheap to start."

Both Mack and Lisa laughed. Lisa was the first to comment on that. "For Mack and I, Roy, it'll just be a good way to get rid of some of it. Sometimes I think Mack would be happier if we were dirt poor, rather than have all that money in the bank."

Ben spoke up next. "Sometimes I feel the same way. Theresa and I have way more than what we need or want. We've been looking for the best ways to donate some of it anyway. This will be a really good way to do use up some of it."

Wanda was next. "That leaves us, Roy. With the money you've been making since you started up your trading ways again, after you teach our friend Sue Sartor the ways of the trading game, we can afford to do our share."

Roy smiled. "I guess that does it then. I'll talk to the right lawyers today, so we can get it going."

Now it was Mack's turn again. "No Roy, I don't think that is it. You've got a great idea, but it doesn't go far enough. Between us, we've got a considerable amount of money to invest in this. I think we should expand on your idea, and buy up several homes. We can turn them into something a lot better than the living hell that Heavenly Homes calls nursing homes. And with Medicare overpaying for that kind of care now, we should at least break even on the deal."

"You know what, Mack, I think that's a great idea," Roy told him. "How about the rest of you?"

The consensus was one hundred percent yes.

"That's great," Mack said. "Now since we all trust each other, I'll have the bank set up an account today that we can all deposit to or draw from. Roy, you'll take care of setting up the corporation?"

"I will."

"Good. Do you other three mind starting the search for houses we can convert?"

They all agreed, but they all knew that Theresa and Wanda had more time, and the truth be known, more knowledge of housing in general. Especially what they'd need for their project.

Mack agreed to the next step, and gave into Lisa's insistence that she come along. Dave and Elaine quietly listened to Mack when he told them there might be a solution to their constant problem with the nursing home people.

Elaine looked at Dave before she spoke. When she did, it was with a voice filled with relief. "Whatever solution you come up with, Mack, we'll do it. Dave's been carrying a huge burden, since I'm no longer able to help as much as I should. I'll be glad to see some of that lifted. Especially now, since Kathy will be gone so long."

Her last comment surprised Lisa and Mack. Dale hadn't said anything to them about his wife, who was Dave's daughter, Kathy, being gone. They instantly hoped everything was okay between them.

Rather than push Dave or Elaine for more information, they decided to ask Dale, since he was Kathy's husband, when they got to the office. A place Lisa was already late for. Mack wasn't, because he wasn't required to check in every morning the way other deputies were. This morning, however, he would check in. He knew he wouldn't accomplish much until he knew what was going on.

Dale was waiting for them when they got there. Rather than comment to Lisa about being late, he immediately said, "Kathy's going on a six month concert tour." Kathy was an up and coming singer with a recent hit record album. "She doesn't particularly want to, but with the sales of all aspects of her music going nuts, she believes she owes it to her recording company and her fans."

"That's some good news," Mack said, "I guess."

Dale smiled. "It is. I'm going with her." That shocked Mack and Lisa. They were left momentarily speechless. "I'm taking a leave of absence. I thought about you as my replacement, Mack, but..."

"I don't know what the but is, Dale, and I don't care. There's no way I want the job. I think I'm a fairly good deputy, but I'll never make a good sheriff. The job calls for talents I don't have, and even if I did have them, I'd have to spend too much time doing things I've no desire to be doing."

"I know that, Mack. Although you're selling yourself short. You'd make a great sheriff."

"Have you picked someone else out for the job?"

"Not on my own, no. It took a while to settle on someone, and when the county board and I did, we were all surprised. The person picked was chosen for some new reasons, along with all the standard reasons for picking a sheriff."

"I hope," Mack said, "you picked someone from your staff. Someone who's actually qualified."

"We did. And I believe that you of all people will agree that she is qualified."

The fact they'd picked a woman surprised Mack. But not as much as the woman they picked did.

"Lisa," Dale said, "how do you feel about being the sheriff for the next six months?"

For Lisa, the shock of that question was so strong that she literally took a step back. Dale smiled at her reaction

"Me?" she asked, her voice showing her surprise. "Why would you pick me?"

"You've surprised the hell out of me too," Mack said.

"Experience is the main reason. While you were helping out in the office, you were practically running it by the end of the first week. You've been in several tight situations since you came on as a deputy, and handled every one of them better than could be normally expected, even from a veteran deputy. And we all believe you are more than capable of handling the job."

"Are those the only reasons?" Mack asked.

A sheepish grin crept over Dale's face. "There's one more. Everyone knows who Lisa is since she made her last arrest. The way she handled that put her out there for everyone to see. She's as well liked as any of us could ever hope to be."

"Can I think about it," she asked, then looked into Mack's eyes.

"Only for a little while," Dale told her. "Otherwise, your hesitation will make it look like you're afraid of the job."

"Well, damn it," she complained, "I am. A little anyway."

Mack didn't have to think about it. She was different from him when it came to holding a position like that. It was true that it was early in her career in law enforcement for her to take it on, but he knew it would be great experience for her. And even if she didn't prove to be as good at it as Dale, he knew the job she'd do would never be something to cause either one of them any embarrassment.

"Take it, Lisa," he said. "I know you can do it, and I'm fairly sure you'll like doing it."

"Do you think it'll be okay though, with you working for me. I'm not yet half the deputy you are. It's going to feel awful strange telling you what to do."

"Actually, Lisa, you're a lot more than half the deputy I am. Sometimes you're a better one than me. As far as you and I dealing with it, it'll be easy as long as while you're on the job, you treat me the way Dale does, and only give me orders that are truly required."

"Mack's right," Dale agreed. "If you let Mack be Mack, you two won't have any problems."

"Okay," Lisa agreed. "I'll do it."

CHAPTER 8

When Lisa woke up and realized what she was facing, she wanted to stay in bed and hide. But it only took a few moments for excitement to overcome her fear, and she quickly left the bed to ready herself for the day. She wasn't sheriff yet, it was her first training day, but the thought of what it was the beginning of was a lot to look forward to. Almost as much for her to be excited about, was telling the family at breakfast. She knew it would be a huge surprise and that there'd be a lot of comments.

"So what's new in the world of law enforcement?" Roy asked his often asked question when Lisa and Mack joined everyone at breakfast that morning.

"A lot more than you're going to believe," Mack answered. "The sheriff's department is going to be looking at some major changes." He smiled, enjoying the fact he was drawing out the news about Lisa becoming sheriff.

"Really," Roy said. "What kind of changes?"

"Dale is taking a six month leave of absence so he can go with Kathy on a world concert tour. The county board has already appointed the new sheriff to fill in while he's gone."

"That wouldn't be you now, would it, Mack?"

"It wouldn't," Mack answered, his smile growing. "There's no way I want the job. I never want to go any farther than being a deputy. That's the place I can do the most good."

"Who's the new sheriff then. Is it anyone we know?"

"It is. You know her really well. I think she's going to make a great sheriff. I told her that when she learned she'd been appointed, and I told her that again this morning."

It took a moment for everyone to pick up on what Mack had just told them. Telling her that this morning meant it could only be one person. The first to respond to that was Wanda. She looked at Lisa, pointed at her, then threw her hands in the air.

"Incredible," she shouted, then rushed to Lisa and gave her a big hug. "This is one of the best things that's ever happened," she loudly proclaimed. "Finally, a female sheriff. And even better, she's in our family."

Theresa quickly followed Wanda with a hug and congratulations. Ben and Roy were too shocked to immediately respond. Ben did first. "Hard to believe," he said. "Long overdue, but still hard to believe. And I agree with Mack. You're going to be a great one, Lisa. You've already proved that you have all the stuff it takes to be one."

Roy finally spoke up at that point. "I agree with Ben and Mack, Lisa. You'll be a great one. My only question is, what do you think about it? Mack's obviously really proud of you, but how do you feel about it?"

"I'm excited for the chance. I also very much appreciate that I'm being given the chance. But it scares the hell out of me too. Filling Dale's shoes isn't going to be easy. He's been an awful good sheriff."

"He damn sure has," Roy agreed, "but you've got everything it takes to do it. All you have to do is your best, and it'll all work out fine."

The confidence they showed in her bolstered her own, and helped make her first training day a smooth one. After that, she seemed to fall naturally into the requirements and responsibilities of the sheriff's position.

She knew how she wanted to run the department, so she was ready to make some changes on her first day on the job. Most of them were minor enough so they didn't have any appreciable effect on the staff. The biggest change was to her new job.

She had no intention of spending the bulk of her time in the office. Like Mack, she much preferred to spend her days out and about, being active in the community. And having the experience of working in the office, she knew what changes were needed to allow her to do so.

The best part of those changes was the fact that several people in the office were given added responsibility. An opportunity they'd long ago earned. So rather than any of them thinking their positions were being disrupted, they were for the most part pleased with the changes.

There was one exception, and that came from a deputy. He thought he was special. Lisa didn't. She knew, from dealing with him a few times on the job, that he was one who always did the minimal possible. Never anything extra.

With a total lack of finesse, he barged into her office. "Before you get too big headed, thinking you can boss us men around," he said, "you'd best know, it ain't gonna work. I ain't never gonna take no orders from you, and there damn sure ain't no way you can force me to."

"I have no intention of forcing you to do anything," she calmly responded. "Other than tell you to get out of my office."

"Do you really think you can make me?"

"If I have to, yes, of course I can. But you will be far better off if I don't have to do it."

He knew then, from the tone of her voice and the look on her face, that she would do exactly what she said she would do. He also knew that he'd made a big mistake by threatening her. He turned to leave her office.

"You can leave your gun and badge on my desk on your way out," she told him. "You're fired."

"What? You can't fire me. You're not the real sheriff."

"Not only are you an arrogant fool, you lack common sense. The truth is, whether you like it or not, I am the sheriff. And, you are fired."

"Sheriff or not, you still can't fire me. You need to have cause to fire me. You don't have any."

"You're threatening me is cause enough. Especially added to the fact you're barely adequate on the job."

"You can't prove I said anything to you. And if you claim I did, I'll deny it. Your word against mine. So, it'll turn out to be you trying to throw your weight around, just because you're the first female sheriff. It'll be you who looks bad."

Lisa smiled and pointed to the front of her uniform shirt. "They don't show unless you're looking for them," she moved her finger close to the body camera she was wearing, "but they do a good job of recording. I turned mine on when you stormed into my office. Deny whatever you want. I have your threats recorded. So leave your gun and badge on the way out."

"I'm going to get you for this, you bitch!" he snarled on his way out of her office.

She ignored him, and as soon as he was out of her office, she downloaded her camera to her computer. She then copied the file to a CD to be doubly sure she had it if she ever needed it.

A second deputy, Jay North, who worked with her in the office, knocked on her office door, then joined her. "He was really pissed. He wanted all of us to leave with him. What the hell happened?"

"Did anyone go with him?"

Jay smiled. "No one. No one in this office would consider it, Lisa. You're pretty well liked here, and we all want you to have every chance at making this a success. None of us much cared for him at all. So what pissed him off so bad?"

"He came in here threatening to never take orders from me. So I fired him. The one thing I mostly don't need this early doing this job is his kind of insubordination. If I let him get away with his threats, it would be over before I ever got started."

Jay shook his head in agreement. "Is it okay if I explain what happened, if someone asks."

"Sure, and if anyone further questions the truth, you can tell them I had my camera on."

"That was good thinking on your part. I'll get the word out."

When Jay left, Lisa thought for a while about firing the insubordinate deputy. On one side, she could have been a benevolent Sheriff and let him off with a warning. On the other side, if she'd done that, she knew that most of the males in the department would have seen it as a sign of weakness. She knew she'd get enough of the weakness claims no matter what she did. So, she decided that she'd handled it properly, and it didn't matter what the deputy did now, he was going to stay fired. In the end, even without the incident, he was a lousy deputy.

Before the day ended, she got more proof of the wisdom of her decision. As the word of Lisa's handling of the incident spread among the deputies in the field, there was nearly a hundred percent agreement with her decision. All the female deputies agreed with it. One of the males thought she might have been a little more lenient.

CHAPTER 9

When the news reached Dell Whitcomb that Lisa was now the acting sheriff, he was visibly upset. He hated her as much as he hated Mack, and felt that life was genuinely unfair for allowing her to have such an important job.

At the same time, he decided to take advantage of the situation. There was no way he could believe she could run the sheriff's department even close to as well as Dale could. That made it a good time to get rid of three terminal patients, to make room for three who would be around a lot longer.

Given that the patients were known to be terminal, he knew that when they died, it was unlikely there'd be autopsies. He also was sure that because he was part of the state's special task force, he could keep any investigation to a minimum.

So, he disabled all the surveillance cameras before he left the home after work, then returned to the home late that night and slipped into the room where the three ladies slept.

The first one he approached was the sickest and was too weak to put up even the slightest defense he when pushed the pillow over face. She died in a few short minutes.

The second was far different. Her struggles were strong as she fought to continue breathing. Her battle somehow turned Dell on, so in the middle of it all he used one hand to drop his pants while he kept her quiet by holding the pillow over her face. He pushed her diaper aside, and proceeded to rape her. It only took him slightly over a minute for his fizzle of a climax to end it.

He finished smothering her, straightened her diaper and his clothes, then proceeded to murder the third lady. It was with a great deal of satisfaction that he left their room. He wasn't worried much about the DNA evidence he'd left behind, because he doubted anyone would ever know what he did. Even if they did, his DNA had never been recorded anywhere, and he intended to keep it that way.

Finally, he knew he could play the role of an extremely surprised person when it was discovered that the surveillance cameras were disabled. All in all, he was sure he'd never be caught for his crimes.

CHAPTER 10

Elaine was feeling better after about with the flu, and was working in the garden when Mack stopped by. As always, she was glad to see him, but because of the still constant harassment from the nursing home people, her immediate reaction upon seeing him was concern.

Dave's reaction when he saw Mack drive in as he was leaving the barn, was much the same. The smile on Mack's face quickly eased the concerns of both of them. Elaine was the first to speak.

"What brings you here on this beautiful morning, Mack?" she asked.

"Some news that I hope you and Dave will take as good."

"That sounds like something serious," said Dave, who was now close enough to them to hear Mack's comment.

"It is," Mack explained, "but like I said, hopefully it's a good kind of serious. It has to do with the solution to the problems you've been having with the nursing home and the special task force."

"We sure could use some help with that," Dave said. "Having that guy arrested sure didn't help much."

"I figured it would only be a temporary stopgap, but what I have in mind now, should be a permanent one."

"What? Are you going to assassinate him?"

Mack laughed. "Nothing that serious. My family and I have come up with a plan to put a stop to their harassment of you, and hopefully, a lot of other people."

"Really? How do you think you'll be able to do that?"

Mack told them of the plan to create assisted living and nursing homes that were actually in people's home or in a place that at least felt closer to a real home.

"Do you think you can actually pull that off. The powers that be aren't going to like it at all. The rich aren't going to profit from it, so they are going to go after you with everything they have."

"I know, but we're hoping to have it up and running to the point it's too late to stop us, by the time they figure out what we're doing."

"It just sounds too good to be true. You're going to lease this place from Elaine, turn it into an assisted living home, hire her as the full time, live-in caregiver for Jill, and pay her a decent salary. To do that you're going to charge us your rates for living here, and for Elaine as the caregiver. Then you will bill Medicare for the charges, which with the new coverages Medicare is now providing will totally cover our costs. So, in the end, we'll just keep on living the same as we always have, without the harassment, and you'll make a profit."

"Yes, which we'll reinvest in more homes. If we get big enough, it will have a negative effect on the corporations like Heavenly Homes. And, along with us making a profit, Elaine will be drawing a salary."

"How can you do this with just Jill as a patient?"

"We can't, and that's the catch. We'll have to add a couple of manufactured homes to the property. Large enough for four actual nursing home patients each. They will be staffed separate, as they will have to be covered 24/7, while Elaine will only be on duty eight hours a day, five days a week. The nursing home staff will assist you on an as needed basis the rest of the time."

"It sounds good, Mack. How long is it going to take?"

"To start, long enough for Elaine to sign the agreements. She has to sign, because her name is on the title of this property. I recommend you have a lawyer look them over before you sign. If you decide to do so after you talk to him, he can serve as the witness to your signing."

"I don't think we need a lawyer," Elaine said. "I can't think of anyone I trust more than you, Mack."

"I appreciate that," Mack told her. "But seeing a lawyer is a good idea anyway. And to tell you the truth, the fact that you go into this with the advice of legal counsel makes it look better for us too."

"Okay, Mack, we'll do it your way."

That's when Mack got a call. He was told to meet the sheriff at the Heavenly Homes nursing home in Kingsburg ASAP. So, he left the paper work for the new deal with Dave and Elaine and went to the nursing home.

A deputy, the sheriff, and Paul Danielson were in one of the rooms when Mack got there. The sheriff, Lisa, looked decidedly angry. In the room were three women lying in their beds. All three were dead.

"None of the medical people have arrived yet to confirm it," Lisa told Mack. "But there's no doubt in my mind that they were all suffocated. Sometime last night. Paul agrees. The one in the middle was raped.'"

"Why the hell would someone rape her. She must be near eighty. And how do you know already that she was raped?"

"Sick, isn't it. The rapist didn't do much of a job straightening out her diaper. So, a nurse here checked."

"If only one was raped, why kill all of them?"

"Be my guess it was so they wouldn't wake up and call out for help. Not that the limited staff here could necessarily respond even if they did. Hell, they didn't report it until a little while ago because they thought the ladies were still sleeping. Over worked as they are, they took it as somewhat of a break."

"Where do you want me to start?" Mack asked.

"Check out the employee records. Then pay a visit to each and every male who was on duty last night. Bring in anyone who you at all suspect could have done this or had any part in it."

"Do you mind, Lisa," Paul asked, "if I ride with Mack. The results are often better if there's two of us questioning the suspects."

"If you think that's what's best, Paul, who am I to argue?"

"Just the boss," he answered with a smile. "Just the boss."

"I'm glad you remembered," she answered, also with a smile. "I still forget sometimes."

"You shouldn't," he said. "You're a good one."

Lisa blushed slightly from the compliment.

Mack and Paul got the addresses of the men they planned to question first, and left the home.

When they got in Mack's truck, he asked, "Do you really think, Paul, that anyone would be stupid enough to commit a crime this serious when they'd be the obvious first suspects."

"I doubt any of these men will be the guilty ones, but we have to check them out anyway. But checking them out isn't why I wanted to ride with you today."

"I can guess why you did. You have questions about Lisa, about Lisa and me."

"I do. On the outside, you don't seem to be bothered about her getting the sheriff's job. I'd have thought you would have wanted it."

"No, Paul, there's no way in hell I wanted that job. I don't have even the slightest desire to be anyone's boss. Nor do I want to spend any part of my days locked in an office. I am where I want to be as far as law enforcement goes. I love what I do now, and I want to keep on doing it."

"I guess that doesn't surprise me, given who you are. But I had to ask."

"What about you, Paul? Wouldn't you liked to have the job?"

"Twenty years ago, I think I would've loved it. Now, I love it that my weekends are most of the time mine. I no longer want that much responsibility. Most of all, I love the relationship I have with my wife. Before you got me up here, I never would have believed we could have what we had when we were first married. Now, in a lot of ways, it's even better than what it was then. So no, I don't want the job. Not now, not ever. I think Lisa's the best person we have for the job. She's already good at it, and she's only going to get better."

"I agree. I've known since I met her that she's smart and strong and able. To come back the way she did after she was kidnapped when she was still a kid shows an inner strength that few of us have. There's only one flaw in her character, if you can even call it a flaw. She has zero tolerance for rapists on any level."

"Again, given what she went through, it's understandable. Add to that, she does have some company with that sentiment. Your feelings on the subject aren't far behind hers, and you and I have no disagreement on the subject."

They spent the bulk of the day checking out and interviewing the men who worked the night shift at Heavenly Homes. None of them struck either Mack or Paul as capable of three murders and a rape.

When they met again with Lisa, they didn't feel any closer to a solution than when they started.

What Lisa had learned was what appeared to be a step closer. Because of the seriousness of the crime, she was able to get a search warrant to go through the homes patient documents, along with all the employee records.

"The three women," she explained to Mack and Paul, "were just recently moved into that room together. By absolutely no coincidence, Heavenly Homes has been after their husbands to move into the home for quite a while. I talked on the phone to all of them, and the home has been putting a lot of pressure on all three husbands. Somehow, my gut tells me those murders were the ultimate pressure."

"Wouldn't it instead," Mack asked, "make the husbands afraid of going into the home?"

"Normally yes, but Heavenly Homes uses the argument that people who refuse to go into a Heavenly Homes facility often have serious accidents."

"It does sound like something those people would do." Paul agreed. "But murdering three patients to gain three patients doesn't quite compute. That's taking an awful big chance for no gain."

"The thing is, Paul, in this case there is potential for gain. The three women were all terminal, their husbands aren't, and they'll require a lot less care. Also, the fact three women were murdered this way might serve as an intimidation factor when people are fighting to get members of their family out of Heavenly Homes."

"I think, Paul," Mack said, "she's got a good theory. Trouble is, how the hell are we ever going to prove it."

"Lots of legwork and digging, the same way police work so often ends up. Now, you and I have to prove we're up to it."

"I think you are," Lisa said. "I want both of you putting as much effort into solving this as possible. And when you can, continue to work together on it."

After leaving the office, they decided to question Dell Whitcomb about the murders and his employees. Two big men, both wearing large smirks on their faces, were leaving Whitcomb's office as they went in.

The man had no intention of cooperating with them and made no attempt to hide the fact. "I have good people working for me," he claimed, "and none of them would hurt any of the guests here in any way, let alone murder them."

"You think then," Paul said, "that someone from the outside killed them?"

"I most certainly do. So, you can leave now, and stop wasting my time."

"We are simply gathering as much information as we possibly can, that might be related to the murders. It's a normal part of this kind of investigation."

"It's no wonder then," Dell snarled, "that you people so often don't solve crimes. Wasting time, the way you are now."

Mack and Paul knew that it was pointless to talk to him any farther. At the same time, Mack now knew that Roy's idea about going undercover as a patient might prove to be worthwhile. When he discussed it with Paul, he agreed.

When they approached Roy about doing it, he not only readily agreed, he was anxious to do it. Life had been good to him for several years now. Where he deeply appreciated that fact, the truth was, he was a bit bored and needed to add a little excitement to his life.

Wanda, after being married to him for a few years, knew he was that way and understood. So even though her approval of him doing it was less than overwhelming, she did approve.

She also had total trust in him, so she wasn't concerned about their friend, Sue Sartor, playing the role of his wife while he was undercover in the nursing home.

CHAPTER 11

With the paperwork completed by the lawyers, the Thomas family's new project was underway. They named the new company Places Of Refuge. It was only two days after the paperwork was complete and they were officially in business, that Dell Whitcomb again showed up to harass Dave and Elaine. The two men with big smirks that Mack had seen at the Heavenly Nursing Home the day of the murders, were with him. Fortunately for those who mattered, it was early evening and Lisa and Mack had just stopped by on their way home after a shorter than normal day on the job.

Mack was in no mood for him, and let it show when he met Dell outside. "You aren't welcome here," Mack told him, "So I suggest you move on, before I move you."

"I don't think so," Dell said, who like the men with him, had a large smirk on his face. "I have all the paperwork required to take poor Jill into custody, and that's exactly what I intend to do. So, step aside. There's nothing you can legally do to stop me."

"Actually, Asshole," Mack smirked back, "I can do plenty. You are trespassing on the property of Places Of Refuge. This is now an official assisted living home. Jill is the occupant of record. All your paperwork, no matter what it is, is outdated. So get the hell out of here."

"You can't force me to do anything," Dell snarled. "I'm a representative of the special task force. You're just a deputy. Also, only an official representative of Places Of Refuge can tell me to leave."

Tired of the man, Mack took hold of his shirt, at the throat, and lifted him until he was standing on his toes. "I am an official representative of the company. Its major stockholder in fact." He pointed at Lisa, who had just joined them. "And she's number one on the board of directors, and doesn't want you here either."

"That's right," Lisa agreed. "And as sheriff of Clayborne County, I also have to warn you that you are trespassing, and if you don't leave right now, I will arrest you."

"We'll just see about this!" Dell proclaimed. "Our lawyers aren't going to like this one bit."

"Too bad and so sorry, but now it's time for you to go."

Stupid as he was, he still knew he had no choices, and left. Not even the big men with him could anything, even though their look showed Mack and Lisa how bad they wanted to try.

"Well," Mack said when he was gone, "the word is out. Be my guess the legal battles will start before tomorrow is over."

"I think you're right there, Mack," Lisa agreed. "But at least we won't be directly involved in those battles. That's what the lawyers get paid for."

"A small blessing, but a blessing nonetheless."

"And in the meantime, Roy will be settling in at their Heavenly Homes place of misery. Hopefully he'll learn enough to put a stop to their constant harassment."

"Better yet, close them down. Now though, Lisa, I think it's time to hire a CEO for our new company."

"Do you have someone in mind?" She asked.

"I do. We want someone intelligent and competent, but not a typical corporate type. Yet, one who can be trained to deal with the corporate side of the business. I think for now, Wanda will be perfect for the job. If she'll take it? And given it won't have to be permanent, I think she might. It'll also give her something to do while Roy's doing his thing. It's a definite that we want someone with a good heart in that job. No one's got a bigger one than she does."

"She's the right kind of person, I agree. But she doesn't have any experience in management of any kind. So, who are you going to find to train her? None of our friends has that kind of experience, and we certainly don't."

"That's all true, but we do know someone who has more than enough experience. And even though he's definitely not suffering from Sainthood, he's a decent enough person to be trusted to do the job we want done."

"For the life of me, I can't think of anyone who fits that description."

"Rodney Twilabee, the CEO of Lands Magnificent. He doesn't owe us anything directly, but it won't hurt him any to do us a favor. Especially given the salary we'll be paying him to train her."

"It sounds like it would work, Mack. Let's talk it over with the family at breakfast tomorrow."

"We will."

"Having Wanda there could stifle the conversation some."

Mack laughed lightly. "In our family, Lisa, I doubt that it'll hold anyone back enough to matter."

Mack intentionally didn't inform anyone that he was going to suggest Wanda for the job. He wanted this meeting to be as spontaneous as possible. He believed their Places Of Refuge business was important enough to put everyone in an uncomfortable, but necessary, position.

So, he and Lisa surprised everyone by getting to Ben's first this morning, rather than their usual last.

"What's up that you guys are here so early?" asked Roy, When he and Wanda got there. He was nearly always the first to comment or ask a question of Mack and Lisa when they arrived for breakfast.

"A fair amount, Roy," Lisa answered. She loved to be the one who responded to his first morning comment, since he always expected Mack to be the one who did.

Mack waited until everyone was at the table, filling their plates, before he approached Wanda with his proposal. "Would you ever consider a full-time job?" he asked.

"I have no idea. I like what I'm doing, so it would have to be something really special to consider it. Since I'm not looking, and I doubt anyone will offer me one anytime soon, I guess it's not a question I have to answer."

"What if someone did come along and offer one? Would you consider it?"

"Well sure, I'd at least consider it."

"The next question is for everyone else here. Would any of you ever offer Wanda a serious and probably difficult job?"

They immediately all agreed that they'd hire her for anything they might need her for. That's when Mack dropped it on them.

"How about as CEO of our new corporation? How about her running Places Of Refuge?"

There was a short term stunned silence. Roy was first to break it. "I'm for it," he said, "but are you sure she can do it, given her lack of management experience?"

Mack answered the question and went on to explain what he had in mind. A stunned Wanda was silent through it all, but her eyes sparkled during the whole discussion. In the end, everyone was in favor of the plan, with one question left. Was Wanda interested.

Her answer was simple. "I'd be honored. Besides, I won't miss Roy so much while he's gone, if I'm real busy. And we've got all the special work needed with the cattle organized to the point it can be done on weekends and in the evenings. Especially if I get some help while Roy is gone."

That left convincing Rodney Twilabee to take on the task of training her. It turned out he was intrigued by the whole idea, and was more than happy to take the job. He also had a suggestion for the company. One that would change the makeup of it.

"I think," he explained, "that the best thing you can do is franchise the business. Do it right, and you'll still be able to control the quality of care, but be free of the day to day responsibilities of that care. Done right, and it can be a win-win situation for everyone. You people who started the company, the people running the day to day operations, and most of all, the patients. And although I know that profits aren't your first concern, it will be profitable. With each individual unit being run by the owner of that unit, it's a natural thing that it'll be more efficient."

Even more ideas flowed from that one, and very quickly they created a smooth-running organization, with Wanda Thomas the CEO watching over it all.

CHAPTER 12

Dell was a very frustrated man. It seemed as though the entire Thomas family was working hard to stop Heavenly Homes from continuing to grow successfully. If it was only the local home it would be one thing, but what they'd started with Places Of Refuge could go national, and that could lead to disaster.

That potential disaster was bringing a lot of pressure down on him from corporate headquarters. The powers that be wanted the problem handled as soon as possible. The problem Dell had was simple. He didn't have anyone who was capable of doing the job.

It took a lot of convincing on his part, but the Corporate heads finally relented and sent a couple of experience men to do the job. Being the professionals they were, they were confident they'd have no problem dealing with a small-town sheriff and her family.

After following their movements for a while, the men were even more confident. So much so, that they believed they could do what they were hired to do almost anywhere they chose to do it. So it was now just a matter waiting for the right moment. Something they were sure was going to be soon.

But even a short wait was more than they wanted to put up with. So they asked Dell to provide them with some entertainment. He knew that if he used any of the professionals he normally called on, it would be too dangerous for them. So he called the one person he knew could provide what he needed.

The girls his brother Darren brought were freshly bathed, but nothing could hide the fact that they were much abused unwilling captives. The girl's struggles did nothing to hold off the two men. They only served to bring additional abuse down on themselves. Before the men were done, one of the girls was badly beaten. The other young girl was dead.

Neither of the men made any excuses for their treatment of the girls. For them, all they'd done is treat unwilling women the way they should be treated. Not to mention the fact that they thoroughly enjoyed doing it to them.

Now they were satisfied. Their waiting time had been filled, and they were more than ready to complete their job they were sure was going to be simple enough.

CHAPTER 13

The more Mack and Paul investigated the murders of the three ladies killed at Heavenly Homes, the more they were convinced they were committed by someone working in the home. The problem was, they had no hard evidence other than the DNA from the semen sample taken from the woman raped. Without further evidence, they couldn't get the court order to take DNA samples from the Heavenly Homes employees. Only hints and innuendos came from the various people they questioned. Finding any other evidence, they knew, was becoming less likely every day. So, they decided to go ahead with Roy's plan.

To make it difficult for the home to check up on Roy, he and Sue spent the first night at a local motel, registering as a couple from Iowa. Even the car they drove had Iowa plates, courtesy of a Minneapolis impound lot, doing a favor for Detective Paul Danielson.

The night was an uncomfortable one for the couple. Where they had a natural attraction for each other, they both knew Roy would never violate the vows he made when he married Wanda. Sue, on the other hand, was equally careful, but mostly out of a deep respect for both Roy and Wanda. Had she lacked that, her approach to the night might have been vastly different.

Early in the morning of their one-night motel stay, Sue called 911, claiming she needed help with her husband, who was suffering from dementia. Given Roy's talent for impersonating all kinds of people, faking dementia came rather easy for him.

When the ambulance arrived, the people who came with it were easily convinced that something was seriously wrong. And even though they couldn't find anything specific, the doctor and nurse in the emergency room agreed. After keeping Roy overnight for observation, he was admitted into Heavenly Homes.

He shared the room he was in with two other men, both in the later stages of dementia. The room was originally designed for only one, so it was too crowded to allow room for any kind of chairs for the men to sit on. Because of that, Roy's roommates never left the bed. When Roy did, the three beds in his room needed readjusting in order to get a wheelchair in far enough to load Roy on it.

He spent long, uncomfortable days sitting in the wheelchair, parked in a hallway somewhere. The monotony was nearly unbearable for Roy, so he gradually started to move the chair. It was the fourth day of moving it before anyone noticed.

The orderly who did, immediately locked the brakes. Roy responds to that with a growl. He waited a solid hour before he moved again. For some unknown reason, that was the last time anyone paid any attention to him.

The only thing Roy could figure, was that they left him alone so much of the time was because the entire unit was severely understaffed and overworked. There also seemed to be an attitude about it. If he wasn't doing any harm, there was no point in taking the time to control his movement. In Roy's case, this was a good thing, but for many patients it was disaster waiting to happen.

Most of the incidents that happened, which ended in injury, were minor. But within Roy's first week at the home, there were two that resulted in serious injury. They both took place well away from Roy, but he learned all about them from simply listening.

The staff at the home, no matter what their position, felt free to talk around him. He was, after all, suffering from severe dementia. Because of this, he often maneuvered himself as close as possible to the places staff members habitually gathered.

Even the manager, Dell Whitcomb, often talked to his favorite employees, the two smirkers, out in the open hallways. Nothing was ever said directly by them, but from their conversation Roy was beginning to sense that they were involved in a lot of the nasties that went on in the home. And Roy didn't have to stretch it much to wonder if they were involved the triple murders. Especially given their attitudes toward any and all of the elderly women forced to live in the home.

The bulk of the people doing the actual caregiving, however, were hard working and cared deeply for the patients they were there to take care of. Given that, well before the end of his first week in the home, Roy was doing the bulk of his eavesdropping on those in the management positions.

CHAPTER 14

It was time for a visit, Mack decided one morning. Even though he'd driven by it nearly every day, he'd avoided a close look at the refuge since the fire. Given how he felt about it, along with his history of trying to protect it, just driving passed the burned-out landscape was heart breaking for him. As much as he knew it was time, he needed to force himself out of his pickup to start the walk.

It rained steadily the previous night, without any wind and only a short period of lightning and thunder. It was enough though, so the scent in the air was clean and pure.

From the road, everything still looks dead and black, but as soon as Mack started walking, new life appeared everywhere he looked. The grass now growing was still relatively short, yet carried a vibrant green. Here and there pockets of wildflowers bloomed in a multitude of colors. Occasionally a standing tree was leafing out. They were all damaged, one way or the other, yet were clinging to life with an almost supernatural will to live.

He had to laugh at a pair of chipmunks when they scurried up the trail ahead of him. They did it in a way that showed him they were simply going about their business, and not running out of any fear of him.

A way into the walk, he moved passed a jackrabbit contentedly chewing on a now huge dandelion plant. Because so much was wide open, Mack could see a lot farther than normal. Off in the distance he saw a lone coyote moving slowly, with his nose close to the ground. He was sure, from the way it moved, it was hunting. He was equally sure that some furry critter or another, probably a few mice, would soon be turned into coyote.

The deeper he got into the land, so devastated by fire not that long ago, the more he could see the return of life in all forms. It made him think about all the people predicting the end of this land as a wildlife refuge.

Surely, they all hoped, everyone involved in rescuing it would now see how hopeless any recovery was. The fire was too devastating. It simply couldn't come back.

They were wrong. It was coming back, and coming back as strong or stronger than ever. Many years would pass, he knew, before it was even close to the magnificent land it once was, but watching it come back would also be something awesome to watch.

Seeing the various critters return as more plants appeared to provide food and shelter, was something that as many young people as possible should see happen. It offered one of the best teaching tools about nature that could be found anywhere.

Long before his walk ended, he was determined to find a way to use the tool. He would need a lot of help to do it, he knew. Yet, he was definitely determined to get the job done. The thought was foremost in his mind as he was nearing the end of his walk.

Then his thoughts were interrupted by something he hadn't expected to see. A small herd of five young deer were browsing on some of the new growth just inside the burned area. Watching them lifted his spirits like little else could.

As it had his entire life, nature once again filled him with hope, giving a meaning to life that he'd felt for a long time he was losing. So, with a new sense of purpose, he drove into Kingsburg to start his working day.

But working day or not, he stopped first at the community garden. Like the refuge, it was a place which could lift his spirits. He got the garden started when he purchased the land it was on after a new local high school was built on different ground. Theresa, his father Ben's wife, coordinated the activity in the garden, which was now growing in full force.

It was especially satisfying for Mack to see so many people of diverse backgrounds working on their small plots without any conflicts, and in most cases helping each other as much as possible.

The garden plots were small enough to be relatively easy to care for, yet large enough to provide a welcome addition to anyone's dinner table. One of the most interesting things going on in the garden was the diversity of crops grown. The plots varied from one growing nothing but salad greens to one filled with several varieties of hot peppers. But most of them were filled with a variety of plants. Although most of the plants in the garden produced something edible, there were enough flowers to fill it with nature's most glorious colors.

As Mack walked through the garden, he was offered food by several people. He deeply appreciated everyone's generosity but had to turn them all down. When he did though, he explained to each individual about Ben, and the fact that along with his vast market gardens, he also had a large plot for the table. All the people who offered food appreciated that he took the time to explain why he turned them down.

When he left the garden, his attitude toward people in general was much improved. If humanity could learn to work together the way the people in that garden did, there might be a chance for the human race to survive. It was something Mack was doubtful of, but this place at least left him with some hope.

So, two things had lifted his spirits this day. A third thing was coming. He was going to have coffee this morning with his wife, Lisa, who was now the sheriff. It seemed as though no matter how much time they spent together, Mack always looked forward to more. Lisa, he hoped, felt the same way. The good thing was, she seemed too.

Another thing he was looking forward to, was the reaction of the working staff at Katy's Kafe, where they were going to meet. Since he'd become a deputy sheriff, he'd met with Sheriff Dale Magee at the same time and place for coffee most days.

It was a bit of a letdown though. Everyone there took it in stride, as if their meeting for coffee was the most natural thing anyone could do. But it took until well into the break that Mack realized how natural their meeting was. They not only worked together, they were married. Why wouldn't they take a break together?

Once they were settled in their booth and had coffee in front of them, Lisa brought up her plans for the day. "The first thing I'm going to do is visit Heavenly Homes. I'm curious about Roy. I want to be sure he's doing okay."

"I was thinking about doing the same thing," Mack said.

"I don't think that would be a good idea, Mack. You don't have a strong resemblance to Roy, but it exists. Seeing both of you there could make people wonder. I know the chance is remote, but still too big a one to take. Add to that, you've had too many conflicts with the place. It'd be best to keep a low profile for now."

He couldn't help smiling at her words. She was right with what she said, and right enough to impress him. She was filling sheriff Dale Magee's shoes as well as they could be filled. And what was so impressive to Mack, wasn't only because she was so young. It was also the fact that such a short time ago, he was looking at her as a very vulnerable girl. Now, here she was, sheriff of Clayborne County. And doing the job equal to any man, and so much better than most, man or woman, could.

Most of the rest of their conversation during their break covered less stressful, topics. So, it was with the most positive attitude Mack had for several weeks, that he opened the door for Lisa as they left. As she stepped out ahead of him, a pickup parked near the front of Katy's pulled away from the curb.

The passenger inside held an automatic in his hand. He started to shoot immediately. Lisa went down. Mack was creased in the arm, but had his gun out almost instantly. Not realizing what happened to Lisa, his return fire was right on. His first shot went through the pickup's passenger's brain, killing him. Mack emptied his gun into the cab of the pickup, hitting the driver four times. The truck crashed into a parked car less than a block later. The driver, still at the wheel, was dead.

It was then that Mack realized Lisa was down and bleeding bad. From her left shoulder and right leg. He immediately called 911. As soon as they were informed of the situation, the air was filled with sirens. An ambulance, which was returning from a previous call, was the first responder on the scene. They quickly took charge of Lisa's care.

Even though he was still bleeding, but knowing there was nothing he could immediately do for Lisa and that hanging in too close he was only in the way, Mack checked out the pickup with the two would be murderers in it. They were total strangers to him, yet seemed familiar. It only took moments for Mack to realize that they just seemed to be very much like the kind of goons Dell Whitcomb surrounded himself with.

Mack's emotions had now gone from a set of renewed positive feelings to an absolute rage. He had no doubt about who was responsible for the shootings, or why they attacked him and Lisa. It was the Heavenly Homes people, and he was sure the responsibility went higher than Dell Whitcomb. In all likelihood, it went all the way to the top of the corporation.

Something that was becoming too common in American business. It seemed to Mack that too many corporations were run as if they were controlled by the mafia. And they might as well be because in the end their only concern was gaining more money and power.

It would be near impossible to prove who was ultimately responsible, Mack knew. Especially to find enough proof for any kind of conviction. But there were other ways to deal with those people, and it was Mack's intention to use every one of them. He would, as much as possible, stay within the law, but...

When he returned to the ambulance, Detective Paul Danielson was there, along with several deputies. They all knew, from the look on his face, not to say too much. All he heard was several, "Sorry Mack," comments, some of them barely above a whisper. Some of the men gave him a light tap on the back, and all of the female deputies gave him a hug.

Without explanation, he gave the keys for his pickup to Paul, and rode in the ambulance with Lisa to the hospital. No one argued about any kind of rules when he got in. He did his best to stay out of the way during the ride, but managed to hold her hand most of the time.

Another good thing about the ride was the fact that he got his arm patched up on the way. And since it only amounted to what was a deep scratch, the patch job was good enough for now.

The wait at the hospital, while they worked on her, felt like forever to Mack. The many people gathered around to wait with him all wanted to comfort him, but knew there was no comfort to give until the doctors returned with the message that she would be okay.

The only one Mack found himself able to talk to was Lisa's father, Bob Anderson, a local dairy farmer. After he explained what happened, and that both perpetrators were dead, Bob said, "I know enough about how all this shit works, Mack, to know what happened wasn't just their idea. Someone else was behind it. Those two clowns were on someone's payroll, and I think we both know whose."

"You're right about that, Bob. I have no idea what I'm going to about this right now. Lisa comes first. But you can bet that something will be done. Within the law if possible. If not???"

When the doctor returned, Lisa's prognosis was close to what Mack expected. She was seriously injured. Her leg wound was superficial, but her shoulder wound was serious. The only good thing was the fact that no bones were hit. Recovery was going to take some time, but her chances of full recovery were very good.

Even though she was under sedation, the doctors let Mack, Bob and his wife, and Lisa's sister and brother see her for a short visit.

As they left her room, Bob again said to Mack, "Don't forget now, you need any kind of help, you let me know. Whoever is responsible for this, one way or the other, needs to pay."

He got the same type of comment from Paul when he went to the sheriff's office the next morning, after his visit with a still sedated Lisa.

"We both know the situation," Paul told him. "The fact is, those ultimately responsible will never get prosecuted. I feel nearly as strong as you do about what needs to be done. There's no way we can let this one slide. They've done way too much harm already. They didn't just shoot Lisa. They also shot the sheriff."

Mack returned his comments with a smile. It was anything but a happy smile, but a smile nonetheless.

As much as he didn't want to do it, Mack took charge of the office. He couldn't see any way out of it. It seemed as though everyone was looking to him for leadership. Even Paul Danielson.

There were no changes in procedure required, because the system Lisa had already implemented suited him better than anything he could create. Then, to no one's surprise, he was appointed temporary sheriff until Lisa's recovery or Dale's return. Whichever came first.

The only good thing about the appointment, as far as Mack was concerned, was that with him in charge of the office, there would be little to no interference with any action he might take against those people responsible for shooting Lisa.

His first stop was going to be the local Heavenly Homes. He asked Paul along, knowing he might need someone with him who could help keep him in check. His emotions were still anything but calm. For him, there was little doubt that he would like nothing better than to beat the manager of the institution, Dell Whitcomb, within an inch of his life.

Doing it, however, wouldn't solve the nursing home problem. The fact was, a large portion of it was caused by those at the top of the business, who were driven entirely by greed. The same greed contributing a great deal to nearly all the world's problems. Those so-called leaders had none of the concern and dedication to the patients in those places that nearly one hundred percent of the actual working staff had. For them, working above and beyond the call of duty was normal.

So, with Paul along, Mack managed to hold his visit to a thorough inspection of the facility. An inspection in which he found many code violations. Rather than write them down, he decided to send in a team of deputies to do a complete inspection, and write a citation for each and every violation. Doing it, he knew, would be a good start to changing some of the things they were doing.

When the inevitable happened, and he checked out the room Roy was in, Roy's performance was perfect. He made absolutely no move that would indicate that he knew Mack. Even though it was a struggle for him, Mack managed to do the same.

For Roy, watching Mack check out his room was a surprise, because it was a fairly strong diversion from the way they'd planned to handle his stay at this Heavenly Home. Sue Sartor hadn't made her morning visit yet, so he hadn't been informed about Lisa.

It was nearly an hour after Mack left that Sue arrived, and another fifteen minutes before she got him moved outside where it was safe to talk. Roy had a difficult time holding his anger back when he heard the news about Lisa.

"There are some son's a bitches in this place," he said, his voice soft, but the anger in it more than obvious, "who are going to pay dearly for that. And when the time is right, I'll be collecting what's due."

Watching Roy, Sue had trouble controlling the shocked look on her face. This was a side of Roy she'd never seen. She couldn't fault him for it, but it was still a shock.

Roy's anger was strong enough to curb his ability to talk any more for a while, so Sue was the first to speak after several minutes of silence. "Are you going to be okay, Roy?" she asked. "I've never seen you like this before."

Roy took a few more deep breaths before he answered. "I will," he finally answered, "but there's some around here who aren't going to do so good. Of all the people they could of gone after, Lisa was the worst mistake they could of made."

"I understand your anger, Roy. But why is going after Lisa the worst thing they could have done?"

"You have to know her story to understand." Roy went on to tell Sue about Lisa's abduction, and how she was repeatedly raped. "She's been hurt enough for a lifetime, without this. So tonight, the revenge begins."

"How are you going to manage that and continue your cover?"

He smiled a wry smile. "I have my ways, Sue. I have my ways."

Watching his face change and listening to the tone of his voice, she could find absolutely no reason to doubt his words.

CHAPTER 15

Ben was the last in the family to learn about Lisa. As it did to everyone else, the news hit him hard. His first reaction was shock, which soon gave way to an uncharacteristic anger. As it did to everyone, he got the feeling that attacking Lisa was the worst mistake they could have made. It also left him with the vow that those responsible would pay for their crime.

Sue joined them for the evening meal so she could tell everyone about Roy's reaction to the news about Lisa. News Wanda was most anxious to hear. Mack only ate a little, and what he managed went down with difficulty. Theresa wasn't able to eat at all, and Ben didn't do much better. He was the first to speak that evening.

"I don't think there's any question about how all of us feel. Someone somewhere has gone way too far. And it's time to do something. Retaliation this time has got to be serious."

"Roy agrees with you, that I can say for sure," Sue said. "I don't know what it is he's got planned for tonight, but there will be some strong consequences for someone."

"However strong those consequences are," Ben said, "don't be surprised. I know my brother well, and I know some of those who have it coming will suffer. And I doubt Roy will limit the suffering."

Ben was right. Roy wasn't going to let any of the guilty off with any kind of warning. If he caught any of them doing what they'd previously been getting away with, when he was finished with them, they'd not simply never want to do it again. They'd never be able to do it again. And for some, being able to function at all would be no simple task.

It was far into the night when Roy started his patrol. As he moved down the empty corridors, he was quiet as a shadow. It wasn't until he was at the far end of the building from his own room that he found one of the people he was looking for.

He was a janitor. One of many doing the nighttime cleaning. His mop and pail were standing outside one of the rooms. He was inside the room, his pants down around his ankles. He was on the bed, leering over one of the younger patients. A woman suffering from Alzheimer's.

"Please," she begged, "don't do that to me again. It hurts."

"Shit," he said, "you're too stupid to hurt. Now spread them legs, so's I can take care of the both of us." With that, he jammed his knees down between her legs.

Roy didn't need any more incentive than that. Silently, he moved behind the man and wrapped his arm around the man's neck, pulling him off the bed. He slammed him to the floor, face down. He kidney punched him hard a couple of times. He groaned as Roy helped him to his feet.

"Who the hell are you?" he asked.

"Someone you don't want to know," Roy told him, then slammed his right hand into the man's gut.

When he doubled over, Roy brought his knee up full force into his face. Not once, but three times. The man melted to the floor, landing on his back. Roy used his feet to spread his legs. His feet were bare, so he couldn't kick the man where he wanted, the way he wanted, for fear of breaking his toes. He turned his back and used his heel. It wasn't as affective as a proper toe kick, but Roy decided it would have to do. To make up for the inferior toe kick, he used his heels on the sides of the man's face. He completes his task with a hard stomp on his nose, making an audible crunch. Roy managed to get out of the way before the blood flow started.

Knowing the building would be filled with chaos when the man was found, he decided to call it a night. He was tucked safely in bed when the lights started coming on. It was morning before he learned there would be rapist, he took care of was in the hospital. It would be weeks before he would return to work, if he ever did.

"One down," Roy thought. "One down and given the institutions shoddy hiring practices, several more to go. You'd think even a shit hole like this place would learn to be more careful about who they hired."

There was little chance of that though. The manager of the place, Dell Whitcomb, had only one concern. Who did it to the janitor? And how did they manage it without being seen or leaving even the slightest trace behind?

He started a search of the entire premises, but it was an exercise in futility. No evidence was found, nor were any suspects. It was, he was sure, the beginnings of problems they surely didn't need.

And he was right. Roy took out two more his second night patrolling. One was a male care giver, and the other was a mechanic responsible for the heating and air conditioning. Both were caught in the same compromising position. The difference was, the care giver was going after one of the nurses. He was sure he could get away with it, because whenever there was a dispute of that sort, Dell Whitcomb sided with the male participant. Any nurse who further objected was fired, then blacklisted.

The nurse involved this time, however, didn't need to complain. The man who attacked was very unlikely to do it again. When he got out of the hospital, his next destination would be as a patient in this very nursing home. And that left Dell short three needed employees.

It was a very unwelcome addition to his already growing list of problems. The worst of which were the many of repairs, improvements, and changes, many of them major, they were faced with. Mack's deputies did a thorough inspection, and after they finished writing all their citations, the fines alone amounted to a considerable sum of money.

When all was said and done, it would be quite a while before that Heavenly Home's nursing home would show a profit. And given the fact that almost nothing upset Dell Whitcomb and corporate management more than losing money, he was an extremely upset individual. So upset that he temporarily called his goons working out in the field, forcing people into his so-called homes, and put them to work inside this building. His hope was to catch the mystery person taking out his loyal employees. Within the first week of the start of his late-night activities, he'd eliminated five employees.

It didn't matter to Dell what those employees might have been doing. All that mattered was the fact that now they were severely shorthanded, and if Medicare learned how short they were, it could further cut into the profits. And that was, in his and upper management's opinion, close to the worst thing that could possibly happen.

Dell's instructions to the goons on patrol were simple. "Catch whoever it is that's responsible, kill them, and get rid of the body."

Roy, however, did not know about the goons when he started his now nightly patrol. He was well away from his room, moving down a long hallway, when he discovered the goons. There were two facing him and two behind him, and nowhere for him to run. The only good thing, a very small good thing, was the fact that those facing him were twice as far away from him as those behind him.

He quickly turned and moved back in the direction he came from. Both of the goons he was now facing were bigger than he was, outweighing him by a good fifty pounds each. He knew his chances of getting passed them were slim, but it was also easy to see that much of their extra weight was fat, rather than muscle. He was also sure from the way they moved, they were slow. The final saving grace, they weren't carrying any weapons.

Roy moved slightly to his left, and faked a kick at the man's groin. He jumped back from the waist down, but at the same time his unprotected head moved slightly forward. Roy slammed the palm of his right hand into his nose, making an audible crunch as it broke. Blood flooded out and as he reached for his nose, Roy did kick him in the groin. This time, after his experience his first night out patrolling, his foot was covered.

The second goon was just beginning to react as the first goon dropped to his knees. Because he was so much faster, Roy managed to land a vicious kick to the side of his knee. It didn't break, but some ligaments were torn loose. As he gasped in pain, Roy threw all his weight into him, knocking him down, then took off running.

The farthest goons stopped a moment to check on the two on the floor. It was all the time Roy needed. He was safely tucked away in his own bed by the time the goons started their search. He knew though, that his time was up at the home.

The next morning when Sue came for her visit, Roy let her know from preplanned signals, that it was time to leave. So, when she took him out for a ride in the wheelchair, they diverted their walk to her car, and left the place. No one noticed he was missing until it was time to go to bed.

CHAPTER 16

When Sue joined everyone for breakfast the following morning, she thought it would be her last visit with them for a while. She was mistaken. Wanda, now the CEO of Places Of Refuge had plans for her.

"I have a proposition for you, Sue," she said, even before anyone started to eat. "I want you to go to work for me."

"I appreciate that," Sue said, "but I really don't have any need for a job. Thanks to Roy, I'm doing fine on my own."

"I know, but this is more than something as simple as me giving you a job. The truth is, I'm a bit overwhelmed running Places Of Refuge. I need someone l can trust, someone I can count on, to work as my assistant. I think you're that person. And the job pays well. Your salary will be the same as anyone in that kind of position would draw. Even someone in a much larger corporation."

"With you guys just starting out, how can you afford it?" Sue asked.

"The truth is, if I was drawing a salary now, we probably couldn't. But since I'm not, we can afford to pay you a decent salary."

"That's not fair. You're running the company, you should get paid."

"I will eventually, Sue, but we didn't start this to make money. We started it to set some things right. Someday, if I keep doing this, I'll get paid. In the meantime, we do need your help. What do you think?"

"Given all that you and Roy have done for me, I can't turn you down. But I'll only take the job on one condition."

"What's that?"

"Until the company is running smooth enough to pay you, I only draw twenty dollars a month. I don't get paid until you do."

Wanda shook her head in disbelief. She was simply hoping she could hire Sue, no matter the cost. Now she was willing to work for nothing. It would go a long way toward getting everything up and running. So she said, "We have a deal Sue. And I couldn't be happier."

The rest of the family was equally pleased to have Sue working with Wanda. Roy especially. But pleased as he was, his mind was distracted. He had the overall feeling that he'd failed with his mission to learn more about Heavenly Homes, and he was searching for something else he could do to assist Mack. After what happened to Lisa, he was as determined as he'd ever been about anything, to be involved in bringing down Heavenly Homes.

Mack was also as determined as Roy to take down the travesty called Heavenly Homes. That thought was foremost on his mind as he drove to the hospital to visit Lisa.

For the first time since she was shot, Mack found her awake. Even though she was in a fair amount of pain, a wide smile filled her face the instant she saw him. Then, when he got close enough to her bed, she pulled him to her and kissed him. It went far beyond the strength Mack thought she'd have.

"It's good to see you," she told him. "Before I was able to wake up enough to communicate with anyone, I was afraid you were shot too."

"This isn't my first visit, Lisa."

"I know, Mack. But everything's been total confusion in my head until I finally woke up this morning. So, how is everything going for you?"

"A lot better now that you're awake. Now all you have to do is get well enough to take your job back. I'm doing it, and it's damn sure not my favorite way to be spending my time."

"It's kind of funny how that works, Mack. You're the most qualified person, other than Dale maybe, to be doing the job. Yet you're probably the only one who doesn't want it."

"I guess. But I'm still the person who grew up in a simple, quiet country life. I still like that way of life, and I come a hell of a lot closer to that way of life being a deputy, than I could even dream of while being sheriff."

"You and I both know that your living anything that could even resemble a simple way of life, isn't much more than a fantasy, Mack."

Mack couldn't help but chuckle at her comment. "I know," he said. "But it's a nice fantasy. Enough of that though. How do you feel? You were shot twice. That's got to be awful painful."

"It hurts, but not as bad as I would have thought. In fact, I plan to be out of here in a couple of days, and back to work within a week. I don't expect to get out of the office for a while after I do. I will, however, be able to relieve you of that part of the job."

"If you get well enough to go back in the office, you can have the whole job back."

"Not right away, Mack. Not until I can do It all. So I'm afraid you're stuck with it for a few more weeks."

He didn't argue with her about it. But it was a huge relief to him when she was able to return to work, even if it was only back in the office. It allowed him to return to working in the field on a nearly full-time basis, with very little time required to do most of the things a normal sheriff was required to do.

The county was for the most part quiet while she was in the hospital, but on her second day back in the office, things again became active. Mack answered a call from an older couple who lived on the far side of the refuge from Kingsburg. The call said they were being attacked.

And they were. By Dell Whitcomb and three of his goons. Mack immediately called for backup, then checked his body camera to ensure that it was on.

He slowly approached the four men who were none too gently forcing a senior citizen couple to their bus, which was little more than a cage on wheels.

"That's far enough," Mack ordered. "Let those people go, so they can return to their home."

"No way," Dell answered. "I have a court order to take them into protective custody. So, you'll have to back off this time, Thomas."

"Not hardly," Mack answered. "You'll have to show me the order, then I'll decide whether it's legitimate. Now let them go."

"Again, I have a court order. The law's on my side this time. So, you either get out of our way, or suffer the consequences. If you interfere this time, you'll find the weight of the entire task force down on your head."

"There's a couple of things wrong with what you just said, Dell. One, there's no way you or the task force can legally attack me. Two, that's not something you or your goons want to try."

Mack stood his ground, almost wishing they'd try something. He knew, without a doubt, that inflicting some pain on all of them wasn't something that would burden his conscious.

It became a mute consideration though, when two sheriff's deputy's cars pulled up in front of the house. One of them in front of the driveway where the bus-cage was parked.

One deputy got out of that car, with his weapon loosely held by his side in his right hand. Two people left the second car. One was Lisa, wearing body armor. Instead of holding her weapon, her right hand rested on it. The deputy with Lisa gave Dell a look that said, "Anything you might try, will be decidedly unproductive."

Mack gave Dell and his goons a grim smile. "Let them go. Now! Or you damn well will wish you had."

Dell again tried to argue. "I have a court order." It was a useless gesture though. His goons had already let the couple go.

Dell opened his mouth to argue more and paid for it. The lady he and his goons had been holding quickly moved up to him, then slapped him with a force so strong it snapped his head to one side. The two male deputies moved to control her, but before they got to her, she managed a kick which landed perfectly between Dell's legs. He instantly grabbed himself as he dropped to his knees, moaning loudly.

"Sorry about that, sheriff," she said. "But his so-called court order says we are too old and decrepit to take care of ourselves. I just wanted to show him how non-decrepit we are."

Her comments drew some serious head shakes from the three goons, smiles from the sheriff and deputies, and deep groans from Dell.

"Okay," Mack said, "the fun's over. You three," he pointed at the goons, load this asshole up. You've got five minutes to get the hell out of here, or all four of you will be spending the night in county lockup. It will be a night you won't enjoy."

They left quickly. As soon as they were gone, Mack instructed the couple to pack enough clothes to last them a few days. They would get lost somewhere in the Place Of Refuge complex of homes, until all the paperwork required to keep them out of the hands of Heavenly Homes was completed.

This couple, Mack was sure, could be easily accommodated. The house next to theirs was for sale. Since both homes were good sized, the two of them together would, with a little remodeling, make a good assisted living complex.

After a short explanation of Mack's ideas, they not only approved the idea, they were excited about it.

It wasn't until they were safely taken care of and settled in a place where Heavenly Homes couldn't get at them, that Mack confronted Lisa.

She just smiled when he did. "I know you're upset, Mack. You're concerned about me. The thing is though, I really feel good now. Good enough to do something like this, and good enough to take over the department Monday."

Mack couldn't argue with her, but his concern was still enough to keep the smile off his face. That is, until she laughed.

"One more thing, Mack, that I'll be taking care of."

"What's that?"

"You'll have to wait until tonight to find out. This one has nothing to do with work."

He finally smiled.

CHAPTER 17

After some discussion, it was decided that for the next few weeks Lisa would primarily stay in the office. If she did venture out, it would only be if she was riding with Mack or Paul.

The first on-the-job ride Lisa and Mack took together proved to be worthwhile. Worthwhile, that is, for three unfortunate young ladies from Minneapolis who were reported missing a few days before, along with another young girl abducted from somewhere in Wisconsin.

Mack and Lisa were out on the far reaches of the county, cruising a little used, very narrow two-lane dirt road. They were there, more to enjoy the beauty of the drive, than to look for any crime. It was something they felt they could justify, given the long hours they'd been putting in.

An old, abandoned farmstead still stood deep into the drive. It was a place they'd stopped many times in the past, but hadn't done so in months. They decided to this time. It always brought back the feeling of an earlier, simpler time. A time most people hadn't lived and so didn't have a memory of it. Because they'd both grown up on farms, they at least had had a taste of that simpler life. The fact that the farms they grew up on were very different didn't matter. They both provided much of what the now mostly gone country life is about.

As soon as they turned onto the long driveway, even before they could see the old farmhouse, they both realized someone was there. There were fresh tire tracks in the dirt, and a few low, overhanging tree branches had been pruned. Mack immediately stopped.

"This is probably something completely innocent," he said, "but I think it'll be good idea to go the rest of the way on foot, so we can get some idea of what's going on before anyone knows we are here."

"I couldn't agree more," Lisa said. "I also think we should put the vests on."

"I won't argue," Mack answered. "We've both been shot enough. At least, for a while."

Lisa couldn't help but smile at his comment, even if it was a grim smile. "Do you think we should call for backup?" she asked.

"Not yet," he told her. "Not until we have at least an inkling that we need some."

Guns drawn, they each took a side of the driveway as they moved closer to the farm house. The trees along the way gave them sufficient cover, so they were still out of sight of anyone in the house when they saw the two white vans parked in front of the old house.

Both vans were without markings of any kind. They were cargo vans, and therefore without any rear windows, save the one in the very back. To Mack, their presence was suspicious. The vans weren't something teenagers would be driving. And teenagers were what he'd initially thought he'd find there.

He motioned to Lisa to stay in the position she was in, then quickly moved up behind the closest van. There was no movement from the house, so he crept over to a window that, he knew from past explorations, was in the living area. Even with the amount of experience he had as a deputy sheriff, what he saw inside the house shocked him. He immediately called for silent arrival backup, using the text option on his cell phone.

He ordered a lot of backups actually, which he knew he'd need to rescue the four young ladies locked in what appeared to be dog kennels. The cages weren't built to hold people, so they weren't high enough to stand in. They weren't even high enough to sit up straight in, so all four of the girls were lying on their side, curled up in a fetal position. None of them wore clothes of any kind. Two men suddenly appeared. Both were in their underwear and obviously sexually excited.

"Which one this time," the smaller of the two asked.

"Don't matter," was the answer he got. "We'll use 'em all, 'for we're done."

Still not wanting to make any noise, Mack texted Lisa, telling her to stay where she was. Next, he moved back toward her, knowing there was nothing he could immediately do to stop the two men. He hated it, but knew he needed to wait for backup. He was lucky though, when he made it back without reaction from the house. Lisa's face was filled with concern when he arrived.

"What's the situation?" she immediately asked.

Mack told her.

"Do you think, Mack, that we should wait for our backup?" she asked. "A lot could happen to those girls, even in the short time we'll have to wait."

"I know, but if we go in now, and the odds against us are as bad as I think they are, we could easily do more harm than good. So as much as I hate to wait, I think it's our only option. We don't want those girls hurt anymore, than they already have been."

"I know you're right. I just hope nothing happens to any of them while we wait. It's terrible what men like that do. They don't deserve to live, if they're doing what I'm sure they're doing."

As Mack watched the look on her face, he realized she meant what she said about them. "I don't think you should go in with us. Given you haven't completely healed yet, it really is best if you wait it out here."

"I understand how you feel, Mack. I really do. But I'm the sheriff now. I can't stand back and send anyone into that kind of danger, unless I'm willing to face it with them. I'm going in."

Mack sighed, knowing better than to argue with her. With her determination, he knew that there wasn't anything he could say or do to change her mind. He also knew that most of his arguments he would use to keep her out of the attack on the house were sexist in nature. They were arguments he'd never use on Dale, simply because he was a male. Most of all, he knew that wanting to keep her out of it was nearly all personal. He loved her and didn't want to lose her, as he had too many others in his life. So he took a deep breath and resigned himself to the fact that this was something he had no choice but to learn to live with, no matter what it did to his own psyche.

Backup began arriving minutes later, but they were very long minutes for Lisa and Mack. For Lisa, the wait was long primarily because of her concern for the girls in cages. She'd been in a similar situation once, and knew what they were going through. For Mack, his concern was for Lisa first, then the girls, and finally everyone going into the old farmhouse. The chances of gunfire were strong, and the last thing he wanted was to see anyone get shot. Anyone other than the perpetrators of this crime, that is.

As Lisa, Mack, and the rest of the deputies moved into place prior to the attack, it became apparent that whoever was inside was either confident in their safety, or too stupid to keep watch. In the end, both were proved to be true.

Mack and Lisa led the attack, moving into the living room where the girls were with the loud crash of the front door. The two now nude men were still in the room.

One of the men was on the floor on top of one of the girls, raping her. The second man was standing close by, obviously excited by what he was watching, and holding himself in one hand, with a gun in the other.

Without the slightest hesitation, Lisa shot the man committing rape in the head, killing him instantly. Even before he toppled over, she turned to the second man, her gun aimed at the lower part of his stomach.

"Drop it," Mack yelled at him before Lisa got the chance.

He foolishly lifted his gun, pointing it in Lisa's direction. Two other deputies were now in the room. They fired at the man with the gun at almost the exact time as Lisa and Mack. They all fired twice, every shot hitting the man. He was dead instantly.

Gun fire could be heard from other parts of the house, but only lasted a few moments. When everything settled down and an inventory was taken, a total of five men were dead. No deputies were even wounded.

A boy, who was only fifteen years old, was found hiding in a closet. He was the son of one of the dead kidnapper/rapists. Lisa had him taken into custody, rather than turn him over to juvenile authorities.

The girls were rushed to the hospital, with a female deputy riding in each ambulance. Lisa wanted them protected from any possible danger, but she also wanted to be sure they were available to be interviewed after they'd been treated and consoled.

No one ever made any kind of a comment about the man Lisa shot without giving him any warning. Right or wrong, there was zero sympathy in the department for the man. He was a human trafficker and a rapist, and therefore to be held in total contempt. In the opinion of the entire sheriff's department, those men in that house, and all people who did what they did, deserved absolutely no quarter. Ever!

The feelings about the boy found in the house, however, were mixed. Even Lisa was less than sure on how to handle him. Mack was the only one who was sure what should be done with him. So, when everything was done that needed to be done with paperwork, etc., Mack questioned him.

The boy was anything but cooperative. As soon as Mack sat him down, he glared at Mack and said, "You killed my pa. Someday, I'll kill you for doing it."

"What makes you so sure I killed him."

"I see you do it."

"You saw me do it? Hiding in a closet, you watched me kill your father? That's quite an imagination you have. What room was your father in when he was shot?"

"The same one I was in."

"Are you saying that he was in the closet with you."

"No. My pa wouldn't hide from no white nigger like you. He fought you guys. I bet he killed a bunch of you too."

"The fact is, he didn't. No one from law enforcement was even wounded."

"That ain't no way true. My pa and his pals were too tough for you to do that. You ain't nothin' but a dumb pussy cop. You can't beat nobody."

"Nobody other than your father and all four of his buddies. They're all dead."

"You're lyin'. They can't be dead. I bet it's them goddamn whores what's dead."

"The girls are all fine, and are now being taken care of."

"I don't believe you. And it don't matter what you say to me, or what lies you tell, I ain't stickin' around to hear no more a yer shit. I'm outa here now." The kid stood to leave.

"You can sit your sorry ass down," Mack told him. "You are going nowhere."

"You can't hold me, I'm a juvenile. That makes me innocent from what my pa or those other guys done."

"The thing is, Kid, you're being held as an adult. You didn't have any ID on you when we found you, so we have no idea of your age. Since you were there with those kidnappers and rapists, we can only assume you are one of them."

"You know I ain't old enough to be no adult yet. You're violating my rights."

"You're old enough to commit rape, and that's all I need to know for now. You're going to be with us for quite some time. And if you don't tell me your name and who your father was, you'll end up with the county, in the general population. And even someone as dense as you should know how popular you will be there."

This scared the kid. "Okay, I'll tell you. I'm Kerry, Kerry Whitcomb. My pa is Darrin Whitcomb."

"Do you have any relatives I can contact, anywhere around here?"

"Just my uncle." Kerry's voice was becoming slightly shaky as his confidence waned

"And who is he?"

"Dell Whitcomb. He's Pa's older brother." At the mention of his uncle's name, some of Kerry's confidence seemed to return. "He's one guy you can't mess with. He'll have me out of here in no time."

"I wouldn't count on it," Mack told him. "I don't have any doubt that you are guilty of enough crimes to keep you locked up for a very long time. Rape is a serious crime. A crime I know you're guilty of."

"That ain't true. I ain't never raped nobody. Sure, maybe I did screw some of them girls, but when I done it to 'em, they loved it. It ain't no rape when they wanted it and liked it."

"You admit it then? You had sex with them?"

"Yeah, but only if they wanted to."

"Then why did you always hit them when you did it to them?" Mack had no way of knowing the kid hit them, but guessed from the kind of person he was that he did.

"Well, they were all whores. Whores always like sex better when it's rough. Besides, it made them lay still, like women is supposed to."

That was enough for Mack. After Kerry made his phone call, Mack locked him in his very own cell. A cell Mack intended to keep him in until he had all the evidence, he needed to have him tried as an adult.

Because the phone call Kerry made was to Dell Whitcomb, Mack waited for him to show up to get Kerry out. And that didn't take very long. He arrived with a lawyer, who demanded Kerry's and his father Darrin's release.

"Can't do either one," Mack explained. "Darrin's dead, and Kerry's being held for rape and suspicion of murder."

Mack added the suspicion of murder charge because shortly before the arrival of the two men, two bodies of young women had been found buried near the old homestead where the attack on the human traffickers occurred.

"He's a juvenile," the lawyer claimed. "And he will be treated as such. I want him released now."

"Do you have a picture ID, along with his birth certificate with you?" Mack calmly asked.

"Don't need it," the lawyer snarled. "You have our word that he is who he says he is."

"Not good enough. Now get the hell out of here and don't come back without his proper identification."

"You're going to regret this," the lawyer threatened. "Before this is over, I'll have your badge."

That was all Mack could take. He laughed. Hard enough for the sound of it to carry throughout the entire office. And that called Lisa and a couple of deputies.

"Is there a problem, Mack?" she asked.

"No, sheriff," Mack answered, still chuckling. "I just couldn't help it when this jackass said he was going to have my badge. It's such a pathetic response to this kind of situation."

"That it is," Lisa agreed. She glared at Dell and the lawyer. "I suppose you're going to threaten to have my badge too. Well, go for it. In the meantime though, get the hell out of my office before I throw you out."

Dell stepped in. "I can guaranty one thing," he claimed. "You won't be sheriff for long in this county. I carry a lot of weight and have a lot of influence here, and you, Lady, are done."

"We all know what kind of influence you have, Dell. Thing is, no one here either can stand the smell of it nor gives the first damn about it. Now get the hell out."

They finally left.

CHAPTER 18

As anxious as they were to interview the four girls who were held captive at the farmhouse, Mack and Lisa knew that it would be better to give them a little time before they did. So, they returned to the scene of the crime, which was becoming an even more serious crime scene. A total of three gravesites had already been discovered. Each had contained the body of a young woman.

One of the bodies was very recent. She'd been strangled and the marks left on her neck by the perpetrator were still clear. As soon as he looked at them, Mack was sure who made them. He looked at Lisa while pointing at the marks.

"What are they telling you?" he asked her.

"They were made by someone with small hands. It could have been a woman."

"They also could have been made by a very young male. Now, who could that be?"

"You don't really think it was Kerry, do you, Mack?"

"The truth is, I'm fairly sure it was him. We'll know when all the forensics have been completed. They should be able to get the fingerprints of whoever did it, and if he raped her, he probably left DNA evidence behind too."

"He's so young. How could someone so young do something like this?"

"You've seen enough to know the answer to that. If you raise a child the way he was raised, he isn't likely to turn out any other way. His uncle is nothing but total evil, and it's likely his daddy was the same."

The search continued, but no more bodies were found. A collective sigh of relief ran through them when the search was ended. The Clayborne County Sheriff's Department was fairly large for a rural sheriff's department, but events of the day would prove to be all it could handle.

Lisa, Mack, and the rest of the department were very aware of that when they finally ended the day. Even after a somewhat unsettled nights sleep, Lisa and Mack woke up in the morning feeling the pressure from the need to solve the crimes they now faced.

So it was with troubled minds that they joined the family for breakfast. As often happened, they were the last to arrive at Ben and Theresa's.

Roy took one look at them. "It must be big trouble this time," he said. "The two of you look like you've been run through it pretty good."

"That's an understatement," Mack answered. He told Roy and the rest of the family about the events of the previous day.

"So," Roy said, "you think the kid murdered the last girl?"

"Until I'm proven wrong, yes I do."

"Are you going to be able to find enough evidence to prove it one way or the other?"

"It would be unusual if we didn't."

"I'm curious, Mack," Roy smiled as he asked. "Would a confession from the kid help."

Knowing Roy as well as he did, Mack knew right away that Roy was dreaming up something. "Of course it would, and I'm hoping to get one next time I question the kid."

"What if you could get one without having to question him. A recorded one, freely given."

Mack couldn't help himself. He smiled. "I think I know where you're going with this, Roy."

"I figured you would. Before you say no, hear me out. I feel like I let you down at Heavenly Homes. I'd like to make up for that failure. But more than that, the kid, if he did it, belongs in prison. Not in some juvenile detention center. And you know damn well that if anyone can get that kid to talk, I can."

It was time for Lisa, given she was the sheriff, to intervene. "How do you plan to get his confession, Roy?" she asked. "You aren't thinking about any violence, are you?"

"Absolutely not. I'll just get him talking. Talking enough so that when he tells me what you need to know, he won't even know he's doing it. I'll be wearing a wire the whole time, so you can be listening in, to be sure I don't cross any lines I shouldn't."

Lisa looked at Mack. "You know better than I about things like this. What do you think of Roy's idea?"

"Roy's pulled off this kind of thing before. Let's give it a try."

"When?"

"How about today. We'll put Roy in the cell just before the noon meal. Give them some kind of treat, which Roy can share with the kid. Give them a good start toward their newfound friendship."

Roy changed into the clothes he wore the previous day, to make him look as if he was in a rough condition. They put him in the cell with Kerry about forty minutes before noon. Mack gave him a push as he went in, to give credence to the idea that the sheriff's department didn't like Roy.

"Damn cops," Roy complained as he sat down on one of the two bunks in the small cell. "One of these days some cop is going to push me when I can push back. World will be less one cop that day. Be a pleasure to do it too."

Kerry smiled at Roy's words. He'd felt uncomfortable and rather lonesome in his cell all alone, so company of any kind was welcome. Having a cellmate who apparently hated cops was a definite added bonus.

"You don't like cops?" he said to Roy.

"You can damn well believe that," Roy answered. "Hated 'em since I was a kid. Wasn't more'n about fourteen when a cop arrested me and got me put in juvy fir nothin'."

"That's what they're doin' to me," Kerry complained. "They claim I raped some women. Never did. Them bitches liked what I done."

"How about that," Roy grinned. "They done got me for the same thing. They say I raped the bitch, which I didn't. It's true, I did rough her up a bit, but the rest of it, she wanted more'n I did."

"Yeah, them whores like it when you rough 'em up. I don't mind doin' it neither. My ma, she taught me. When we done it, she always wanted me to slap her around after. She kind of liked it when I choked her some too. Said it was like punishment from God, for doin' it with her kid."

"That's right. That's what most of 'em want. Punishment from God for doin' wrong by givin' away their bodies. So givin' 'em what they want kind of gets to be a habit, don't it."

"The slappin' them around does." Kerry stopped talking a moment after heaving a big sigh. He shook his head the way a person does when they recall a pleasant memory. "But the chocking, that was always special. I only done that with the special ones."

"What made them special?" Roy asked, knowing he was getting close to the confession they were looking for.

"Mostly it was them what was older, sort of like my ma. I liked them best. The last one was especially good. After, I didn't want no one doin' it with her no more. So, I fixed it so she couldn't."

"And how the hell did you manage that?"

Kerry sighed again, a soft smile spreading over his face. "I choked her. It was easy to do, 'cause

I enjoyed doin' it. At the same time, it was kind of hard. She fought me at the end."

"What the hell did you do with the body? Cops find bodies, they get awful damn curious."

"That weren't no problem. We buried it out in the woods by where we was stayin'. Cops ain't never smart enough to find stuff like that. They never did find ma neither, after I done her. And me and pa just buried her in the back yard where we lived then. We just planted some flowers there."

"You did your mother? That's kind of a hard way to be, ain't it?"

"Not really. The last time she done it with me, she said we wasn't to do it again. Too big a sin, she said. I couldn't just let her quit on me like that. I know she'd be doin' someone else besides pa. That wasn't right, so I killed her. She didn't fight so much though. I think she wanted me to do her. She was always kind of sad like."

"What did your pa say when you did it?"

"He like thanked me. Said it saved him doin' it."

That was enough for Roy. Tough as he was, listening to Kerry talk was actually making him sick. But he'd accomplished what he set out to do. They had a confession. And it wasn't quite lunchtime. So, Kerry didn't get his treat.

They also had a problem. After the forensics on the five dead men and they were all identified, they discovered that Kerry's father wasn't one of the dead men. He'd somehow escaped.

They did have enough information about him, however, to get a search warrant for his most recent address. There, they found and dug up the grave his wife, Kerry's mother, was buried in. Her autopsy proved that she'd been strangled.

There was no question now, about Kerry's fate. It mattered not whether he pleaded guilty or went through a trial for the murders, he was destined for prison, serving time with adults.

At this point, most of the legal system considered this chapter of the crime to be mostly over. Not Mack. His instincts told him there was still a lot to be done. At the top of the list was finding and putting away Darrin Whitcomb, the man who was Kerry's father and Dell Whitcomb's brother. And the place to start the search was keeping an eye on Del.

Doing that, brought to the fore another ongoing problem. The constant harassment of Dave Sanders, along with Elaine and Jill, the people he lived with.

CHAPTER 19

Dell Whitcomb was sure he'd get his way this time. He had new papers from a well-paid judge, Judge Mathew A. Barker, ordering Dave and Elaine to turn over Jill to him. Dave was waiting for him when he and his three goons got out of their car.

"I don't care if you've got some more phony papers," Dave said, keeping his voice calm. "I don't care about anything you think you can do or anything you want. You're getting nothing here. Especially not Jill. So, turn your ass around and get the hell off this property."

"I have an official court order which orders you to turn Jill over to us. We are here to enforce these orders. We will take her by force, if force is proven necessary." His words were followed with a broad grin.

Dell loved what he was doing and what he thought he was going to accomplish. Getting even with Dave was incredibly satisfying for him. Even better, he was sure taking Jill would upset Lisa and

Mack Thomas. Two people he hated as much as he was capable of hating.

Dave stood his ground, knowing that it would only be a matter of minutes before help would arrive. As soon as Dell and his goons pulled into the driveway, Elaine called Lisa on her private cell phone line. Lisa responded immediately and ordered all cars in the area to converge onto what was now A Place Of Refuge property.

Dell started to move in on Dave, with his goons right behind him, when the first of several sheriff's deputies arrived. She was a veteran deputy and was wise enough to have her gun in her hand when she left her car. A gun she immediately pointed at Dell.

"Be a good idea for you to back off," she said to the four men who badly wanted to beat Dave senseless.

Dell shook his head no. "You can't legally shoot us," he claimed. "We are simply fulfilling a court order. So, by law, you have to put your gun down and let us do our duty."

"Not hardly," she answered, her contempt for him dripping from her words. "So back off before I'm forced to shoot you. You have a record of harassment of these people, so my shooting all four of you to stop that harassment is justified."

"We'll just have to take that gun away from you then," Dell snarled. He looked at his goons. "Take her gun," he ordered.

The goons started to move in on the deputy. She ordered then to stop. They didn't, so she shot the one in the lead, purposely only creasing his left arm.

He screamed in pain. The other two each took a step forward, believing they could rush her before she could fire again, when two more deputies arrived. At the same time, Elaine burst out of the door with a twelve-gauge pump in her hand, which she fired into the air.

"I won't be aiming at any arms," she yelled. "Heads will be more like it."

A new, relatively young, male deputy was in the first of the two cars that had just arrived. He wasn't sure what was happening, but he knew that Dave, Elaine and Jill were friends of Lisa and Mack, so he was mentally prepared to do whatever it would take to protect them. Even so, his gun hand shook slightly as he pointed it in the general direction of Dell and the goons.

The sheriff's department's detective, Paul Danielson, was in the other car. Without hesitation, he walked up to Dell, pushing one of the goons out of his way as he did.

"You never learn, do you, Idiot," he told Dell. His anger was so strong that his voice was filled with a hissing sound, similar to a very large snake. A snake coiled and ready to strike. He grabbed Dell's arm and spun him around, cuffing him.

He put cuffs on the goons next, then called an ambulance for the goon who was shot, and still slightly bleeding.

"I have a court order," Dell screamed over and over again.

"Have is the wrong word," Paul said finally. "It's past tense now." He tore Dell's court order into quarters, handed the pieces to Dave, and said, "Find a place to burn this bullshit."

Dave gratefully took it then, deciding as he did that the garbage burn barrel was as good a place as any to do the job.

They were loading Dell and the two undamaged goons into separate cars when Lisa and Mack got there. It surprised everyone when they got out of Mack's truck. Lisa was the driver. Letting someone else take the wheel of his pickup was something Mack just didn't do. But now, it was a good illustration to everyone as to how much trust Mack had in her. He wanted everyone in the department to know that wife or not, he had total faith in her ability to do the job she now had.

And she didn't hesitate to take charge, equal to anyone else who had ever held the position of sheriff of Clayborne County.

Everyone there from the sheriff's department appreciated her ability to take charge and make decisions as they were needed. And they liked the fact that she did it without the hesitation sometimes afflicting people as young as her, who suddenly found themselves in a situation similar to the one she was now dealing with.

But the people most impressed by her were Dave and Elaine. They didn't hesitate to tell her how they felt either. Once the Heavenly Homes villains were loaded up and on their way to jail, that's what they did.

"I'm impressed," Elaine said first. "There's no doubt about it. You are meant for the job. You come across every bit as good as Dale. And he's the best sheriff this county ever had."

"I'm every bit as impressed as Elaine," Dave added. "You are exceptional at what you're doing. I am concerned though about what kind of trouble you might be getting yourself into, defying a judges court order."

"I'm pretty sure that court order isn't even legal," Mack answered.

"Legal or not, it's flat out wrong," Lisa added. "And Judge Barker, the one who wrote the order, is out of line. I'm also nearly positive that he's on the Heavenly Homes payroll. I don't have any time for judges who break the law. More than anyone else, they are supposed to represent and uphold the law. So, I consider it an even bigger crime when they break the law, then I do when other people break it."

For Lisa, her attitude toward judges went beyond them simply breaking the law, it was also personal. When she was kidnapped years before, one of the men who paid to rape and beat her was a judge. That had a profound effect on her appreciation of those who sat in black robe on their courtroom pulpits and judged others. It took a lot for her to put trust in any of them.

It was only a couple of hours later before her mistrust proved to be well founded. As soon as Judge Barker learned that the people who represented the corporation that provided him a large portion of his income were under arrest, he issued an order that they be released.

He had a problem though. He couldn't legally do it without a hearing. Something he couldn't instantly schedule, due to lack of space and personnel to hold court. Some of the people who might have been available, suddenly became unavailable. He wasn't the most popular of judges, any more than representatives of Heavenly Homes were popular among seniors.

Normally, the average person didn't get involved in legal matters of this type. But Heavenly Homes had already harmed so many seniors, that most people, if not directly touched by their activities, had heard the stories about them. Stories universally bad.

This suited Lisa and the rest of the sheriff's department just fine. They'd already installed Dell and his goons for hire in their cell. It was supplied with one open toilet, one drinking faucet, and four metal cots covered with thin mattresses. It measured eight by ten feet. Not much space for four men.

Lawyers were called, but there was little they could do before there was a hearing, due to the seriousness of the charges against them. They were attempted home invasion and attempted kidnapping. Charges that did have a small chance of sticking, given the judges court order was unjustified. It was now an impasse, a waiting game, for all concerned. The only good thing about it was the fact that it was the Heavenly Homes people who were locked up in their now crowded cell.

CHAPTER 20

After all the sheriff's department, along with the Heavenly Homes people, were gone, Dave finally went inside the house. What he found there was every bit as disturbing to him as the trouble he'd just been through.

Elaine was struggling to move Jill from the couch she was sitting on to the commode next to it. The problem was the fact that Jill was suddenly no longer able to hold her head up, and the way it dropped back behind her, threw everything out of balance. They also couldn't be sure, because Jill was no longer capable of communicating one way or the other how she felt. But it looked to them that it probably was painful for her.

Dave sighed heavily at the sight, even as he moved to assist Elaine. Once they got Jill settled on the commode, they discovered they'd been too slow moving her. He assisted Elaine as she did a complete change of clothes, along with a new diaper, on Jill.

After they finished, and had Jill again safely situated on the couch, they went into the back bedroom to talk. They didn't want Jill to overhear them. They felt that she was facing enough, without hearing their concerns about her too.

"This doesn't look good, does it?" Dave said.

"No, it sure doesn't. But we've known for a long time this kind of thing was coming. Everyone we've dealt with, doctors, nurses, whatever, have warned us that it was inevitable."

"I know. This and more. She's never going to get better. It's just going to be a steady downhill run. But knowing it sure as hell doesn't make it any easier."

"No, it doesn't. Taking care of her is simply going to get more difficult as time goes on, and she constantly gets worse."

"One thing though, Elaine, no matter how hard it gets, no strangers are ever taking over her care. We take care of her until it's over, no matter how hard it gets."

"I wouldn't have it any other way, Dave."

"The one saving grace in all this, is having Mack and Lisa such good friends. I know they're just doing their jobs the best way they know how, but I often get the feeling that they're always making an extra effort to look out for us."

"The truth is, Dave, that's exactly what they're doing. If it weren't for them, Jill would be suffering in the Heavenly Homes nursing home. We owe them a lot for what they've done."

"We do. I sure do wish there was a way to repay them."

His wish was something that neither Lisa nor Mack would ever have expected. They never felt as if anyone, let alone Dave or Elaine, ever owed them anything. Doing the work they did was reward enough. More than that, they had more money than they ever wanted, not to mention, needed.

On this night though, they did need something. A decent night's sleep. It was another exhausting day. Even so, Lisa felt another need. It was actually the same need Mack felt, but he didn't want to let it show. He felt that Lisa was already under enough pressure. She didn't need more, at the moment, from him.

Lisa, on the other hand, had no qualms about putting that kind of pressure on him. So, after her shower, as she got ready for bed, she tried to decide which of her nightgowns would have the strongest effect on him. After a few minutes of indecision, she decided she was too tired to decide something so complicated, and wore the one nature provided.

From Mack's point of view, it was his favorite, and served to accomplish what they were both yearning for. The only problem, if one could be foolish enough to call it a problem, it meant sleep came for them much later that night.

The problem again occurred in the morning, so it also made them late for breakfast with the family, even though they did wake up with plenty of time to spare. And as always, Roy teased them when they did join the family at Ben and Theresa's.

It was Lisa who was the target of his humor. "My, but you sure have a glow about you this morning, Lisa," he said. "You must have gotten a good night sleep."

His comment didn't phase her. "That's right, Roy," she answered with a broad smile. "We both had the kind of nights sleep that would please anyone. Even an old man like you."

Her answer gave everyone a laugh. When it stopped, Roy's wife, Wanda, said, "Thank god, even if he is old, we still manage that kind of sleep now and again."

They all laughed again and felt better for it. Given the stress level of the various activities they were all involved in, the laughter was a much-needed release.

Even Ben and Theresa had been feeling stressed from their extra responsibilities. Along with their normal work, which already filled most of their time, they'd been overseeing all the work that needed to be done to keep the ranch running smoothly.

Normally, Roy and Wanda took care of all the ranch work. Now though, Wanda was the acting CEO of Places Of Refuge, and Roy had been doing his undercover work for the Sheriff's Department.

"So, tell me," Roy said, "What's happening with law enforcement that you two can afford to sleep in this morning?"

"Truth is, Roy, we probably shouldn't have, given all the things going on. Yesterday it was Heavenly Homes again, with another court order, from the same Judge Barker again, trying to force Jill into their hell hole for seniors."

"She's already in one of our homes," Roy complained. "So why the hell would any judge issue a court order to force Jill into one of their dumps?"

"Because that's what he's getting paid for."

"Then he belongs in jail."

"We know that," Lisa interrupted. "And he would be if we could prove that he's taking bribes. Trouble is, we don't have a way to do that. There's no way we'll ever get a search warrant to check his financial records. No judge will ever issue one on a fellow judge."

"What would you say to my getting some proof of his misdeeds, then dealing with him my way?" Roy asked. "If you got a confession out of him, it ought to go a long way toward solving at least some of your problems with Heavenly Homes, shouldn't it?"

"You plan on doing something illegal, Roy," Lisa asked, but with a smile.

"Not exactly," he answered. "Not anything you'll ever have knowledge of anyway. And I guaranty, nothing I do will be violent in any way."

"Okay, Roy," Mack said. "Do whatever you think you can do. But whatever it is, I think it's best neither Lisa nor I get involved. Time comes, however, Judge Barker is ready to confess, we'll be glad to get involved."

Roy just smiled, looked at Wanda, winked, and took a sip of coffee. Mack and Lisa concentrated on the plates of food Ben set in front of them. There was less than normal talk the rest of the meal, and what there was, was all about growing vegetables and the current price of beef.

CHAPTER 21

After Mack dropped Lisa off at the office, he cruised around the county, the same way he'd done most mornings since he became a deputy sheriff. Without realizing it, he soon found himself on the main county road running through the wildlife refuge.

It had been a while since he was there, and he immediately saw the changes that were rapidly taking place. Most of the land that was meadow before the fire was becoming green again. Native grasses were pushing their way up through the ashes. And since the recent rains provided enough moisture and the ashes provided the fertilizer the grasses needed, they stood out in brilliant shades of green.

Scattered among the grasses, were ever increasing numbers of broad leaf plants. Many of them were flowering in a multitude of colors. The few trees that survived the fire were now fully leafed out, and occasionally they held perching birds of various species.

For Mack, this was life as it should be. Wildlife of all kinds coming back from a devastating fire, without the help or interference from humans. Not simply surviving, which was more than the world of conservative commentators predicted but returning with all the glory the earth can provide. That is, when there weren't humans involved to screw up that ability.

As he looked around, mesmerized by the natural beauty around him, he was suddenly hit, like a heavy hammer behind the head, with memories of what the refuge he was now studying once was. Along with all those memories, came the painful ones of the people lost. As always happened when the memories returned, he thought of Mandy, the woman who would have been his wife. And Linda, his friend and lover. The women murdered by people just like the people now running Heavenly Homes.

Mandy and Linda were murdered, and recently they'd tried to kill Lisa. Someone Mack loved as much as he could ever love anyone. So, he knew then, that whatever Roy was planning, he would have Mack's full support. As much as Mack respected the law, he knew that always trying to follow it to the letter was a fool's errand.

In this world, the one that now was so much controlled by the conservative rich and powerful who cared for nothing but extending their wealth and power, it was sometimes necessary to use the few methods available to maintain at least some semblance of sanity and human decency. Even if those methods weren't always virgin pure.

The feelings Mack was filled with became so strong that he was forced to come to a complete stop. He parked at the side of the county road to regain control and clear his eyes enough to focus. As he concentrated on bringing himself back to his surroundings, he failed to see the black, SUV driving up on him. If it hadn't been for the young doe that ran out in front of the SUV, forcing it to swerve and kick up a dust cloud, he never would have noticed.

Without thinking, without knowing why, and certainly without analyzing the situation, he unhooked his seatbelt at the same time he reached for his gun. As he did, he looked into the side mirror on his side of the truck. Something was poking out of passenger side windows, both front and back. He didn't need to let them get any closer to know what those objects were.

Without time to do anything else, he fired at the vehicle. Even though the chances of it carrying innocent people were extremely slim to none, he shot out the front tires rather than the windshield. The SUV was moving just fast enough, so that the driver lost control when both tires flattened simultaneously. It veered toward the deep ditch running along the left side of the road. When the left front tire went over the side, the car flipped and landed on its top. All four men inside managed to scramble out.

Three of the men were armed. The fourth, who was driving, immediately took off running across the open field. Because there was nothing he could do, Mack let him go. He knew that if he started shooting at him, he would lose the control over the other three men.

"Best drop the guns," Mack told them. Two of them did. The third one made the mistake of thinking he could shoot faster than Mack. He was wrong. Mack put two bullets into him. One in each shoulder. Wounds he hoped wouldn't be lethal. He was more than tired of all the recent killing.

It did little good though, toward saving lives. One of the other two men, still armed with an automatic that was stuffed in his back belt, pulled the gun and fired. In his haste, he missed. He didn't get off a second round. Mack's return fire destroyed the man's heart.

As Mack cuffed the one sensible and still unharmed man, he asked him, "Who was the one who ran? A good friend of yours?"

"Not hardly. That chickenshit son of a bitch was Darrin Whitcomb. About as gutless a man as you could find, no matter how low the gutter you were lookin' in might be."

His answer left Mack wishing he had taken a shot at the man. He was one person Mack very much wanted to get his hands on. But it was too late now, so he put in the calls to get the support people and waited. And while he did, he did his best to stop the bleeding from the shoulders of the first man he shot. It was more than he could do though, and the man bled out just a few minutes before the ambulance arrived.

It was a completely disgusted man who explained to Lisa and Paul what went down just minutes later.

"Don't blame yourself for any of this, Mack," Paul told him. "You sure as hell didn't invite those people to do what they did."

"I know, but I am tired of it all right now. I'm about ready to become a full-time cattle rancher."

"You don't think, do you? that in today's environment, anybody's going to let you do that? There's just too many of the evil ones out there to ever let either one of us quit."

"I know. That doesn't stop me wishing for a better time though."

"It doesn't stop any of us from wishing for that. But bad as it might be, we've still got a lot of worth working for, and hard as it is sometimes, worth fighting for. And no one has fought a better battle than you have, Mack. So, no more talk of quitting. We need you."

Mack looked at Lisa, who stood there silently while they talked. She didn't have to say anything. The look in her eyes said enough. It gave him the strength he needed to pull himself together, and soon he was ready to face whatever the world was going to throw at him next.

That next thing proved to be close to the last thing he ever wanted to hear. As soon as he started to question the only man, they had in custody from the four, the dreaded news came out of his mouth.

"Before you get to harassing me too much, Thomas," the man said, "I got to tell you something. You got to watch that pretty little wife of your's."

"What do you mean by that?" Mack asked, his anger over what he thought the man was accusing Lisa of written all over his face.

"Now hold on. Just hold on, Thomas. I can see by your look, you think I'm sayin' bad about her. I damn sure ain't."

"What the hell are you saying then?"

"What I'm meaning to say is, you got to watch her. You know, protect her. I know I'm no good for much, but I ain't into hurtin' women. Not the way some others is. I especially ain't when they're as pretty as the one you got."

"That's just fine," Mack said, the gruffness in his voice dominating it. "You like pretty women. But what's that got to do with me watching her."

"Darrin Whitcomb is what watching has got to do with it. It's true he's about as chickenshit as a man can get, but he's got it in his head that it's his mission to kill her. And he's mean as they come. Especially with women. He won't quit now, not until he rapes and mutilates her first. The rest of those what hired us to do you in, they just want the two of you dead. Real dead."

"Why are you telling me this? In doing it, you just gave me your confession."

"I know. But you got me dead to rights anyway. I ain't gonna get out of this one.'

"I still don't understand why you're telling me all this. Even without me asking a question. For the most part, people like you damn rarely, if ever, try to do the right thing."

"Truth is, that's pretty much who I've been most of my life. I ain't had or seen much good in livin' since my wife was raped and murdered about twenty years ago. A cop done it. He got away with it too. That is, until I killed him."

Mack shook his head as he watched the man. Tears were welling up in his eyes. It was the last thing he'd expected to see.

"Thing is, Thomas, there was one thing I still cared about. My wife and me, we had a son. I didn't do too good a job a raising him, but I did try. So when I lost him, well, I pretty much gave it all up. That's part of why I'm talking to you now."

"If you gave it up when your son died, why were you involved in coming after me today."

"'Cause that's when he died. Today. You shot him."

"I'd think you'd hate me then, not trying to warn me to watch out for my wife."

"Mostly, I would be. But what you done, and the way you done it, well, it was the most decent thing I've seen in a long long time."

"I hate to admit it, but I damn sure don't feel like I did a damn thing decent today. I did what I had to do, but decent, no, nothing."

"Thing is, you did. The first one you shot. Any other cop would have killed him right off. You had no choice but to stop him, yet you went out of your way to try not to kill him. Then when the shooting was over, you busted your ass to save him. I saw the look on your face when he died. You actually cared."

"Was he your...?

"Yes, he was my son, but because of what you done, and the way you done it, I can't in no way ever hate you, Thomas. So, watch your wife. I'm pretty sure she's worth a lot more than just watching."

Mack couldn't answer. This man had just told him something he definitely didn't want to hear, but not at all as a threat. Instead, it was a simple act of kindness, thanking Mack for his own simple act of kindness.

CHAPTER 22

Roy got busy with his latest undercover job for the Clayborne County Sheriff's Department. Finding out as much as possible about the financial dealings of Judge Barker, who was on Heavenly Homes special, secretly recorded, payroll.

Like a lot of people in his generation, Roy was mostly computer illiterate, so he definitely didn't have the skills required to hack into those accounts. He did, however, have a friend who had the skills. Sue Sartor was a techie of the first order. She could make a computer sing and dance, and there wasn't much online she couldn't get into if she had a mind to do it.

She also knew how to accomplish her mischief in way which was close to impossible to trace. Bank accounts were relatively easy to access for information. Stealing money from them was more difficult. Since information was all that she and Roy were looking for, she didn't need to use up much time getting into the Judge Barker's accounts.

Because the judge was constantly moving money from one account to another, and conducting nearly all of his business online, Sue quickly had a mountain of information for Roy. He profusely thanked her for her efforts.

"No big deal," she answered. "After all you've done for me, Roy, what I did for you today is small potatoes."

"No, it's not. It's a big deal. I just wish there was some way I could repay you."

"Like I said, you already have, in hundreds of ways." What she didn't say, was that there was something she wanted from him. And that was Roy himself. Her feelings for him started shortly after they met, and time had constantly strengthened them.

She didn't act on those feelings now, anymore than she ever had, or ever intended on doing. She couldn't, given the amount of respect she had for both Roy and Wanda. That respect, and the certain knowledge that Roy and Wanda would never separate, would always keep her silent.

"Even if I have in some ways helped you, you can believe that there'll be a lot of thanking going on tonight when we go through all these records."

It wasn't until evening, after Ben and Theresa fed them all supper, that they started. It didn't take long to find what they needed to prove the judge was taking in a lot of illegal money. Exactly where the money came from was another story. Much of what Heavenly Homes and the judge did was on the stupid side, but the money part was all in cash.

So, for the moment, it was a wait and see time. They knew that they'd eventually have to get the right financial information from Heavenly Homes. Hacking into their records would be more difficult, and dangerous, then going after the judge was.

There was no doubt though, about going after them. They all knew there was no real choice. Left unchecked, letting them continue could only lead to disaster for many people. First and foremost, among the people they were concerned with were the uncountable seniors now being forced into their deadly institutions, called nursing homes.

To speed the search for financial evidence against Heavenly Homes, Sue Sartor was told to use part of her workday at Places Of Refuge for that function. To do it, she used a special laptop, using cellular technology, rather than Wi-Fi. That allowed them to accomplish their searches using an untraceable phone line. She also kept the time of her searches short, making it even more difficult for anyone to trace her. And last, when she wasn't working with it, she kept the laptop shut down.

Keeping things shut down was also Mack's priority now. Especially when it came to the dangers Lisa was facing. The fact of being sheriff, was alone enough to attract all too many nut cases wanting to prove something by harming or killing her. Added to that now was the obvious intention of the Heavenly Homes organization to go after her, as well as Mack. Worst of all, in Mack's opinion, was Darrin Whitcomb. He was acting on his own, and was therefore less predictable, which made it more difficult to see it coming when he made his attempt on Lisa.

All of those possible problems meant Mack was forced, as much as anything by his own concern for her, to spend much of his time guarding her, often while she objected to it. That conflict was slowly creating some discord in their relationship. Lisa finally verbally objected to it.

"This has got to stop, Mack!" she told him, in no uncertain terms. "You have to back off. You're interfering with my job, the way you constantly won't let me go on my own."

"I don't like this anymore than you do, Lisa, but it is way too dangerous for you to be on your own right now."

"I realize this job has that element attached to it. You knew it too, when you agreed that I should take it. So, I'm asking you, please back off."

"I can't. What's going on now isn't normal. You are facing far more danger out there right now, then you'd normally face in a year. So, no, I won't back off. Not, at least, until we catch Darrin Whitcomb."

"Damnit, Mack, what you're doing is beginning to affect not only both of our jobs, it's beginning to hurt our personal relationship. That alone ought to be enough to get you to at least ease up on the way you're hounding me. You're trying to control me, and I don't like it. I don't like it at all."

"I can't blame you for that. I wouldn't like it if someone was trying to control me either. The problem is, I can't stop trying to protect you while this is going on. If I did, and something happened to you I could have stopped, I flat out could not live with it."

"So, no matter how I feel or what I say, you're going to continue with this crap?"

"I am."

"Even if it has negative effects on our relationship, our marriage?"

"Yes. You know my history. You know what has happened in the past, when I did back off, just as I was asked to do. That's not going to happen again, no matter what the cost. I love you too much. I'd far rather lose you because you objected to my being overprotective, then to watch you die because I didn't follow my own instincts."

"Damnit, I could just fire you, you know."

"I do. Go ahead. But it won't stop me. We've both been hurt enough, Lisa. You are splitting with me would near kill me, but that's still better than seeing you get hurt, get shot, or get killed."

When he stopped talking, tears were beginning to well in his eyes. Lisa was taken back by the depth of his feelings. Watching him, seeing the determination on his face and the love in his eyes, suddenly evaporated all the negative thoughts and anger she felt when she started their conversation. She dropped her head for a moment, then lifted it and moved into his arms.

"Damnit, Mack," she said softly, "I think I'd die if I ever lost you. I love you with all my heart. I'm sorry. I'll try to be patient with you until this is over."

"You don't have to be sorry. All you have to do is let me keep you safe. I know you can take care of yourself, but in situations like this, you need eyes in the back of your head to be safe. Let me be those eyes."

"Okay." She kissed him, sighed heavily, sat down at her desk, and went back to work.

What Mack didn't see as he turned away to leave her office, were the tears falling on the paperwork in front of her.

CHAPTER 23

It was with a great deal of relief that Mack stopped his truck and turned off the engine. They were safe at home, one more day. And for one more day no attempts were made on the life of Clayborne County Sheriff, Lisa Thomas.

It was the same relief Mack felt at the end of every day. Darrin Whitcomb still hadn't made a move against Lisa, and the direct problems with Heavenly Homes seemed to have eased up considerably.

So this evening, since it was early enough, Mack suggested they take a walk out in the still natural woods and meadow located behind their house. It was a small pleasure they hadn't enjoyed for a few weeks. A longer time then they'd ever gone since they had their house built, shortly before they were married.

Lisa readily agreed, and quickly changed from her uniform into clothes and shoes more appropriate for walking in the woods. She took his hand and held it as they slowly strolled along the single path through the woods.

Along the way, one or the other of them constantly pointed out the various wild creatures and plants they encountered. One of the first animals they saw was a coyote. It was a large male, who was only mildly concerned with them, and so rather than run when he saw them, simply sauntered away. It was almost as if he was saying, "I'm not afraid of you, I just don't trust you."

The small herd of five whitetail deer reacted the opposite. As soon as they saw Mack and Lisa, they exploded into action. All of them leaped high into the air, and landed running at full speed. Lisa laughed at their reaction. Mack smiled, but more at Lisa's reaction than the deer's.

Lisa stopped moving as the deer ran. She looked up at Mack. "These are the best times," she said to him. "Just you and me, out here in a wild place where life is free of all the evil and horror we both see too much of now."

"They are. All my life, I've been able to find a peace in places like this, that I could never find out there with my own kind. It's so soothing and takes away so much of the stress of the day. It's hard to want anything more when we're out here."

Lisa chuckled. "When I was still a kid and I'd come alone to places like this, I'd think about you, Mack. I was so in love with you, even then, when I was supposed to be too young to have such strong feelings. Most of the time those thoughts turned me on completely. Just like they're doing now."

She reached up and put her arms around his neck. "So, are you going to do something about them?

Or are you going to force me to be a kid again? Either way, I'm going to let those feelings have their way with me." She kissed him with passion, then stepped back and slowly unbuttoned her blouse. She wasn't wearing a bra.

He quickly followed with his shirt, now filled with all the same desire as she was. When they finished undressing and joined together, he silently thanked the powers that be for giving him such good fortune.

It was the same good fortune that Dave Sanders once felt he had, but now was something rare. He knew that he'd been lucky to have had the life he'd lived. It was just that dealing with Jill, with her constantly deteriorating health, was stressful. Just as her needed care was 24/7, so was the stress. And with Elaine not feeling near as well or strong as she once did, ever more of Jill's care fell on his shoulders.

Again, as he did twice already during the day, this evening he was giving Jill a complete change of clothes. When he completed the task and had Jill tucked safely in her hospital bed for the night, Elaine walked up behind him and put her arms around him.

"I'm sorry, Dave," she said, "that you're being stuck with her care so much of the time."

"It's okay," he told her. "If it was me instead of her, I know you'd be taking care of me."

"Of course I would. Just like I want to take care of you now. That is, if you're still interested?"

Dave turned to face her. He expected a smile. Instead, he found a frown. "What's the matter?"

"I'm scared. So much has changed. I'm afraid it might all be lost."

"As long as we have each other, it can't be all lost."

"The desire though. I'm afraid it's all gone. I know you love me, Dave. But do you desire me anymore? I'm sure not what I once was."

"Yes you are. You are every bit as beautiful as you ever were. I still have all the desire for you I had that first time. That cold, dark night with the wind howling and the snow coming down so hard it was blinding. Even with a light."

"How could you, the way I sag in all the wrong places."

"I like your wrong places the same as always. It isn't the lack of desire that keeps me from showing you that, it's all because of the number of years I've lived. I'm just not who I once was."

"It's been a while though. Think maybe we could pretend we're young enough tonight."

He smiled. "I don't see any harm in trying."

Soon after they went to bed, the wind started to blow hard enough to howl.

And where the howling wind served to remind them of a younger, better time, it was also made for good cover for the men who came in the night. Not to Dave and Elaine. They came instead to do harm to the Thomas family.

Because they actually knew very little about them, those that sent the men to do their dirty work thought that they would create a major crisis for Mack and his family, simply by destroying a vegetable field, and cutting fences where some of their cattle were pastured.

Had they known, they would have been bitterly disappointed. Mack and Lisa never needed to take a dime out of the profits from the ranch. They were rich beyond anything either of them wanted, much less needed.

Roy and Wanda put nearly all of their share of the profits from the ranch and invested them in improvements to the place. Roy made enough trading to easily support them. And he still had a small income from his ranch in Texas. The ranch where he and Wanda spent most of every winter.

Ben and Theresa were also well to do. Ben was careful with the money he'd made from his huge antique auction, and from the very large salary he made when he worked for Land's Magnificent, so he had no financial worries either. He was still an organic vegetable grower only because he loved doing it, not for the money he made. That money, he gave to charities that helped people who needed help, and to some environmental organizations.

The men who came in the night did, however, create some problems. The fences they cut allowed many of the cattle in that pasture to get out. They were only a relatively small herd of young stock though, and they didn't wander too far. Both ends of the pasture fence were cut, so there were cattle loose in two places.

"What do you think is the best way to round them up?" Mack asked Roy after they evaluated the situation.

Roy thought for a moment, then grinned. "There's lots of ways, Mack, but as long as we got to do it, let's have some fun. Let's use the horses. You and Lisa take one end of the pasture. Wanda and I will take the other."

Neither Ben nor Theresa were much for horses, and Ben could see right away that his brother was going to make some fun out of the mess, so he said, "Theresa and I will fix fence while you four have your fun. Thing is though, we get this done, the four of you can help us salvage what we can from the vegetable field."

Even though they'd ridden less this summer than ever in the past, Lisa and Mack took to it right away. As soon as they began bunching the cattle, they developed a rhythm to their movements. They weren't into their work long before they realized the joy to be found in working cattle the old way, with horses.

Best of all for Mack, was watching the broad smile filling Lisa's face as they rode. Almost as good as that smile, was the fact that it took them a couple of hours to get the cattle rounded up and safely tucked away in the pasture. It was a time of pure pleasure for them, rather than hard work.

They had fewer cattle to herd than Wanda and Roy, so they spent another thirty minutes assisting them. And all through that short thirty minutes, four adults rode horses as if they weren't much older than kids, and all that time, their faces filled with smile.

Once the cattle were all safely put away, they all tackled the vegetables. What initially looked like a near total loss, wasn't nearly that bad. The evil men who were sent to do them permanently financial harm had accomplished almost nothing. They were, and people like that usually are, simply too stupid to know how to do what they were hired to do.

They did accomplish one thing though. They allowed four good people the chance to have more fun than they'd had in a long time. The experience went far beyond the joy of riding the horses. It made them feel young again, and gave them a renewed hope for things to come.

If a planned disaster could turn into such an invigorating experience, it seemed as though anything was possible. It also bought back some of the joy that can only be found in doing simple work. Work that not only gets something done, but fills the heart and mind with complete satisfaction.

When the work was done, Roy said, "Be my guess, if them that tried to ruin us last night knew the truth of what it turned out to be, they'd be more than a little pissed. All the same, I ever get my hands on them, there'll be hell to pay."

"You got that right," Ben agreed. "There isn't much hurt I wouldn't like to give them."

"With some hard work by Lisa and I, along with a bit of luck, maybe we'll all get that chance."

"This time," Theresa said, "I think I'll just shoot them."

CHAPTER 24

Sue continued to devote part of her time digging into Heaven Homes financial records, both local and national. She was finding it far easier to get into the local records than the national. So she was grateful for the help she got from an unexpected source.

Dale Whitcomb was in charge of the home in Kingsburg, and his methods for everything connected with the home were sloppy at best. For the financial end of the business, he had both guidelines and rules to follow. The problem was, he never did any kind of real work if he could find a way around it. Bookkeeping was no exception. If he could find an easier way, that's the way he did it.

So when passwords were needed, he often as not eliminated them. Why should he have to try to remember them, and worse yet, be forced to type them in every time he wanted to perform one simple task or another. So he didn't.

That gave Sue a multitude of easy openings which gave her a digital trail to follow to hack into corporate records otherwise nearly impossible to access. In the end, because of the doors that were opened by the local record keeping, she managed to dig far deeper into Heavenly Homes corporate records then she'd previously expected to.

As she followed their financials, the computer technicians at The Homes central office were beginning to notice some suspicious movement in their records. Initially, they couldn't pinpoint what the movement meant or where it was coming from. It wasn't until they discovered that it originated with the Heavenly Home in Kingsburg, that they were able to put traces on the movement. Traces that only led them as far as the cell phone system, not as far as Sue's cellular connected laptop.

While they were searching for her, she began noticing their activity. It was enough to convince her to stop hacking their records. At least for a while. She was sure the locals would never have the ability to track her down, but at the same time, had no doubts that the computer people on the national level could.

Knowing the dangers of continuing her surveillance of their activities, she immediately disconnected from the net and closed up her laptop. In her haste, she made one mistake. She forgot to power off the laptop. It was still possible to find her. Extremely difficult, but possible.

As she returned to her normal work at Places Of Refuge, concerns over Heavenly Homes people being able to trace her slowly disappeared. She finished her day with nothing out of the ordinary happening, and took her special laptop with her that night without further thought about it. On her drive home she paid little attention to anything going on around her. Once there, she did lock the door when she went inside.

It wasn't until she was in bed, close to sleep, that she heard the crash of the large window in her living room as someone broke in. Keeping her wits, she immediately grabbed her cell phone from the bed stand next to her and speed dialed Roy's number. He answered and all she had time to say before the two men who broke in reached her was, "Someone just broke into my house."

The phones disconnected, so Roy tossed his phone to the now awake Wanda. "Call Mack," he said as he dressed. "Someone broke in on Sue."

Wanda didn't hesitate. Mack answered on the third ring. She told him what Roy said. "I'm on my way," was his only answer.

As soon as he told Lisa what was going on, she called it in and ordered every car at all close to Sue's to move in. When Mack and Roy got there, two sheriff's cars were waiting for them.

"Sorry," said the lead deputy among them. "There's no sign of her here. The only things out of order are the broken window and her bed. It's pretty messed up, like she put up a real strong struggle."

"Damn," Roy said, "this doesn't look good. Have you got any ideas on where to look, Mack," he asked.

"Only one. Heavenly Homes. But to do a complete search, we'll need a search warrant."

"How the hell are you going to get one tonight?"

"Simple. We know a judge who I'm pretty sure can be convinced to give us one."

"That's right, we do. Judge Barker."

The judge was extremely angry when they beat on his door and woke him up. When asked, he refused to issue a warrant. So Mack laid into him, warning the judge about the amount of evidence they already had against him, and all the things they could do with it other than use it in a court of law.

Reluctantly, he issued the warrant. As soon as Mack and Roy left, he started packing. It was time, he knew, to retire to his villa in Mexico. He decided to leave his wife of forty years at home. He had other special ladies waiting for him down there.

At that moment, Mack and Roy didn't care what he did. Their only concern was for Sue. They wasted no time getting to Heavenly Homes but called Lisa on the way. Mack simply slapped the search warrant down on the welcome desk in the homes lobby and started his search.

He took the first floor and Roy took the second. Lisa arrived before either one of them was farther than halfway through their floor. She checked with Mack to start, then she and the deputy who arrived when she did, started in the basement.

Not being much brighter than the typical goons hired by Heavenly Homes, the men who grabbed Sue made little effort to hide her. They held her in a storeroom in the home's basement. She was tied to a chair, and they also didn't attempt to hide her cries when they slapped her, trying to force her to answer their questions.

"Now what's the goddamn password," a gruff voice yelled, just before Lisa and the deputy barged into the room.

Because of their overconfidence, the two men weren't at all ready for them. They thought they could defeat the two women anyway. The deputy defended herself in the simplest way possible. She shot her would be attacker.

The one who went after Lisa wasn't so lucky. She was far more limber, and a lot faster than he was. She easily sidestepped him, and lashed out with her pistol as he went by her. She caught him on the side of the head, then as he fell, she landed a vicious blow to the back of his head. When he tried to get back up, he got onto his knees, but when he tried to push himself up, her strong kick landed directly under his chin, snapping his head back. It didn't break his neck, but did damage it enough to doom him with a lifetime of pain.

Lisa quickly untied Sue, who had sat wide eyed but silent while Lisa did her number on the kidnapper. "You got here a lot quicker than I thought you would," she said, her hands moving to the bruises on her face. "How'd you figure out where I was so quick."

"That was all Mack," Lisa answered as Roy, followed by Mack, hurried into the room. Sue was still in the pajamas she was wearing in bed, so Lisa got her a hospital gown off a shelf in the storage room to cover her.

"Damn, I'm sorry," Roy said when he saw Sue's bruised face. "Are you okay?" He pretended not to notice how revealing her pajamas were.

"It'll hurt for a couple of days," she answered, "but I'll be okay. I think it would be a lot worse if they were after me, but it's the computer they were most concerned with."

"How did they even know about it?"

"I made a mistake. I forgot to power it down, so they were able to trace its location." She went on to explain all of the technical details.

Roy was shaking his head when she finished. "I suppose you actually know what she was talking about," he said to Mack.

"I do," Mack said. "And it wasn't really all that complicated."

"Well, it damn sure was to me. I think I'm going to finally force myself to learn about that shit, much as I don't want to."

They were loading the two kidnappers, one into an ambulance, the other a hearse, when Dell Whitcomb finally showed up, complaining about the disturbance.

"You can complain all you want," Lisa told him. "But if I was you, I'd save my energy for the talk with my lawyer. You're under arrest, again, for kidnapping. There's no way those two clowns could have been here without you knowing it.

"The fact is," he whined, "I knew they were here, but I didn't know why. And you can't prove otherwise."

"I guess only time will tell on that subject," Mack said as he once again cuffed him.

As happened the last time he was arrested, his lawyers tried to get him immediately out of jail. They weren't able to do it. The bought and paid for judge had disappeared.

While Lisa and the deputy took Dell to lock him up, Sue sent her laptop with them for safekeeping. Roy and Mack took Sue to the hospital, just to be sure none of her injuries were serious. She was lucky, and they were superficial. That meant she wasn't required to stay there.

"I guess," she said, "you guys will just have to give me a ride home."

"Not tonight," Roy said. "Tonight, you stay with us."

"I don't want to put anyone out," she argued, not daring to ever tell anyone why she didn't want to stay with Wanda and Roy. Her feelings for Roy were too strong for her to ever want to be in the position where something could happen between them.

"It's not a matter of putting us out," Roy explained. "It's more what we've been asking you to do for us. Now we've gotten you in the position where you could have been bad hurt. So there's no way you're going to stay alone right now."

"I don't know, Roy. It's just not a good idea."

"And why not?"

"That, I can't tell you. Not now, not ever."

"Well hell, I can't let you stay alone."

Mack broke into their conversation. "Would you mind staying with Lisa and me?" He asked. He'd been watching Sue closely, and from the look in her eyes, he guessed what the problem was.

"I don't want to put you out either, but I guess that'd be okay."

So she went home with Mack, leaving Roy confused as to why. He considered Sue to be a good friend, so it was impossible for him to understand why she'd objected to staying with him and Wanda.

It wasn't until they were all seated at the breakfast table the next morning that he figured it out. He was talking to Mack, when he suddenly moved his head and looked at her. The momentary look in her eyes told him. He knew he'd need to step lightly around her from then on.

CHAPTER 25

To no one's surprise, Sue went to work the next morning. They all knew her mindset. She was determined to do all she could to not only support the Thomas family, but also, in her own way be part of it. Her only concern was her feelings about Roy. Part of her wanted to take them to their conclusion, but the larger, wiser part of her told her to avoid that kind of move at all costs.

Mack and Roy were both concerned about what other moves she might make. They knew that anything she did outside of work or Mack and Lisa's home, was potentially dangerous. More than once during breakfast, Sue and Wanda were warned about that fact.

Wanda finally tired of their reminders. "We got the message," she said. "We'll be careful. Sue's riding with me to work this morning, and back here tonight. She goes anywhere today, I'll go with her. I will be armed."

"Good," Roy responded. "Damn good."

Even though she too knew Sue's reason for not wanting to stay with her and Roy, Wanda let things ride for the first couple of hours that morning. Then she asked Sue to join her in her office.

"Since there's no easy way to talk about something like this," she said, "I won't try to make it easy. I know why you didn't want to stay with us last night..."

"I don't know," Sue interrupted, afraid of what Wanda was going to say, "what you're talking about."

"Yes, Sue, you do. First off, I want you to know, I'm not pissed about it. Concerned yes, but angry, no. It's easy to fall in love with a man as good as Roy. And he's been especially good to you, so what's happened is really no surprise. So the question is, what are we going to do about it?"

"The smart thing for me to do would be to continue to deny it. I can't do that to you, Wanda. I've got too much respect for you, and for Roy. I think what the best thing for me to do is leave here now and get on with my life. I'm not looking to do anything with Roy, even if I could. And you and I both know there's little chance of that. He's way too straight arrow to ever do something like that. Not to mention that he loves you too much to ever cheat on you."

"Do you want to leave Sue?"

"No, not at all. I just think it would be best all around. I'd never want to hurt you Wanda. You've been too good a friend. I don't want to screw anything up for Roy either. So I don't think I should stay, even if the chance of anything happening between Roy and me is so slight."

"Do you really think it would be that terrible if something did happen between you and Roy?"

"Yes. Don't you?"

"It depends on how it was handled. If I never knew about it, it likely wouldn't be that big a deal. I'm confident Roy wouldn't leave me because of it. We still love each other too much. If I did know about it, and you didn't try to mess with my head because of it, I could still handle it. I think I know you well enough to believe that if something did happen, that's the way you'd deal with it."

"I still think it'll be best if I leave."

"I don't. I think you should stay. No matter what happens, you've become an important part of our lives. So I think I can speak for all of us, including Roy. We want you to stay."

"That's incredibly generous of you, Wanda. I don't know if I could feel that way if things were reversed."

"I'd bet you could. There's one rule we've got to follow though."

"Whatever the rule is, I think I'll be able to follow it."

"Good. The rule is, Sue, no lies between us. Not ever and not about anything. Any questions either one of us have, get answered. Agreed?"

"Totally. It's as good a rule as we could have between us."

"You are staying then?"

For the first time in a long time, Sue felt as if a huge weight was lifted from her shoulders. Tears were in her eyes, but a big smile filled her face when she answered. "Yes, absolutely yes!"

Sue and Wanda left their chairs and shared a hug, both confident that the friendship they already had was now even stronger than it was. So strong that Sue consented to stay with Wanda and Roy for the duration of the time it wasn't safe for her to be left alone.

When they told Mack and Lisa, they were not in the least upset. Relieved would be a better way to put it. They were still young and new enough in their marriage to appreciate and enjoy their privacy. With company in the house, their nights were always quieter than they otherwise might be.

This was especially true now, with Lisa under the same restrictions as Sue. Everyone from Mack on down, knew that with the constant threat of Darrin Whitcomb, it was dangerous for her to be out on her own. The truth was, it was dangerous for her to be out and about, even when someone was with her.

So, there was a constant tension, not only between Mack and Lisa, but throughout the whole department. Everyone needed to find a way to deal with it.

Mack and Lisa used many techniques to ease it, but the one that worked the best is the one they loved the most. And that was love itself, which could only be expressed as consistently as they did, because they had so many youths and vigor. Not having company at night also helped a great deal.

That didn't help much at the morning breakfast, with Roy being his usual self. It seemed he always had some kind of comment when they arrived late. Something they'd frequently been doing since they discovered their tension release. It helped them to sleep at night, and proved to be a good way to start each day.

"Late again," Roy said this morning. "What I wouldn't give to be young like that again."

"Oh, hell, Roy," Wanda said, "you're plenty damn young enough for me."

Forgetting how dangerous her words might be, Sue said. "If it was me in Wanda's place, I'd wager you'd be enough for me too."

The kitchen went silent. Realizing what she'd done, Sue blushed heavily. Wanda, being the good sport that she was, saved the day.

"Could be," she said, "he'd be enough for the both of us. Not that either one of us would ever want that to happen."

Mack and Lisa smiled at their comments. It ended Roy's teasing. At least, for the rest of this breakfast.

Sue though, felt embarrassed through the rest of the meal. She also felt bad about what she'd done. So, she apologized to Wanda on the way to work.

"There's no need to do that," Wanda said. "The truth is, it's probably better that you did say what you did. In fact, I think it'll be a good thing if we both make occasional comments. It'll keep the whole thing in perspective. And that should help cut the frustrations."

"As long as we don't do it too often. I was awful embarrassed this morning."

Wanda laughed. "I know, and I appreciate it. It showed me that it was a slip of the tongue on your part, and not something to get Roy's attention."

"That's something I'll be avoiding as much as I can," Sue said, taking a deep breath and looking around. That's when she noticed the large pickup following way to close. "There's a truck..." she started to say.

"I know," Wanda answered. "I've been watching it a while. There's a township road off to the right, up ahead a way. Tighten your belt and hang on. I'm not going to slow down before I make the turn. If they follow, we'll know we've got some real problems."

Wanda made the turn with no warning of any kind. The pickup behind them couldn't do anything but keep on going. The driver braked hard, however, turned around, then took out after them.

Wanda didn't fool around and floored her all-wheel drive pickup. It was a midsize, so it was smaller than the one chasing them, but it was equipped with a large V8, and therefore somewhat faster. Instead of the pickup behind gaining on them, it was now falling further behind.

Wanda had the advantage of knowing the roads better, and that also proved to be a distinct advantage on the slightly winding gravel road. By the time they reached the next paved, county road, there was no chance for the larger pickup to catch them.

As soon as they were running smoothly, Sue called Lisa on her private cell phone and explained to her what happened. Lisa, Mack, Paul Danielson, and deputy Sandy Bert, who often worked with Lisa, met them at the Places Of Refuge office.

Rather than wait for another incident, they were there to plan a way to go after whoever was driving the pickup. So Wanda and Sue spent their first working hour planning the way they hoped to trap the latest of Heavenly Homes hired killers.

CHAPTER 26

It was time for Dell to gather his resources together and try to come up with some kind of plan to defeat the Thomas family. Something they'd consistently failed at. The only time they'd even come close was when the men from corporate managed to shoot the sheriff.

And that had proved to be another failure. That damn Mack Thomas killed both of the men, even though they were supposed to be professionals. And the damn sheriff recovered from both her wounds. Another unexpected thing. Especially since she looked so small and fragile. An appearance decidedly inaccurate. She was everything but fragile.

He started the meeting by asking everyone there if they had any decent ideas on how to put a stop to the Thomas family's, along with the sheriff's department's, constant interference with the Heavenly Home's goals.

All of the things they'd done, from blocking the movement of new patients into the home's facility's, to the creation of their competing assisted living and nursing homes, the newest action was the worst.

The entire management team at Heavenly Homes corporate headquarters knew that if all the information they suspected was hacked was ever made public, it would do them serious harm. It could even prove to be fatal. Especially the proof of the many times they'd forced people into one of their homes.

They didn't dare complain to the law about what they were doing. That would create too big a chance of the data going public, the absolute last thing anyone connected to Heavenly Homes wanted.

"You all know why you're here," Dell began when the group settled down. "We've got to figure out a way to put a stop to the constant harassment we've been getting."

"That's for damn sure," Darrin Whitcomb said immediately. "It's getting damn hard to move the girls, with them having their noses constantly poking into everything."

"I'm sure," Dell answered, the annoyance with his brother's comments obvious, "but the corporate problems are far more serious."

"For you maybe, Dell," Darrin whined, "but I need to keep moving them girls. Else-wise, I might lose my connection. I don't want to do that. They pay a premium price when you got American girls to sell."

"If that's the case, then why haven't you taken out the sheriff yet? And her trouble making husband while you're at it?"

"I'm working on it."

"Well, you damn well ought to work harder at it." Dell paused a moment to stare his brother down, then moved on with the meeting. Given the number people they'd lost trying to get rid of the Thomas family, the response from the group was slow. They were aware of how few options they had.

Finally, after much discussion, Darrin agreed to lead a group to first go after Sue and Wanda, so they could get the computer with the dreaded information on it. They felt desperate to know what files Sue managed to download, so that if the information somehow went public, they'd be ready to deal with it.

Once that task was complete, Lisa and Mack were the next target. She was the sheriff who constantly worked against them, and was especially hated by Darrin. They wanted Mack out of the way simply because they knew that as long as he was alive, he'd never let up on them. As far as they were concerned, he was a miserable liberal, who didn't agree with the idea there should be no limit to the amount of money a person made, no matter the cost to the rest of humanity.

CHAPTER 27

This morning, Mack and Lisa were early, rather than late, for breakfast. Roy didn't comment on it. His concern for Wanda and Sue was strong enough to eliminate any other thoughts. They were in affect now bait for the people hunting for them and the computer.

All the information Sue gathered while she was in Heavenly Homes accounts had been backed up several times and stashed in several places. The Heavenly Homes people expected that to be the case, but were desperate to get the computer anyway. They felt they needed to know how much information might be revealed to the public.

The Homes people, not being the type to have original ideas, were waiting for Sue and Wanda in almost the same spot they'd been on the previous day. Wanda took the same evasive action as she did the first time.

This time, there was a SUV blocking the road ahead. Four armed men were inside it, but before they could leave their vehicle, they were surrounded by sheriff's deputies, all with their guns drawn and pointing at the men in the SUV.

Seeing that, the pickup trailing Wanda and Sue attempted to flee in reverse. There was nowhere to go. Mack and Lisa were blocking the road. The driver turned the pickup, so his side of the truck was facing away from Mack's pickup. He leaped from the truck, and bent low, took off running. The ditch on the side of the road was deep, and that gave him some cover. From there, he got into the woods. There was a lot of brush, which he ignored in his desperation to escape.

Mack went after him, and was sure he had the man, when he tripped over a tree root. He hit his head on an exposed rock when he landed. The blow stunned him, and by the time he recovered the man was gone. Mack was disgusted with himself. This was the second time he'd lost Darrin Whitcomb.

Even with the loss of Darrin, they still had five men in custody, and they did it without even one shot being fired. Everyone but Mack was more than pleased with the results of the day. He was still a lot more concerned about Lisa than he could ever be about locking up five criminals.

Because of that, she was on his mind when he started questioning the men they captured. And that mindset posed a problem for him. He definitely didn't want any of them to see how worried he was about her safety. There was too big a chance that the decision makers at Heavenly Homes would find out how he felt and somehow use it against him, and possibly the entire sheriff's department.

He decided to approach them with enough aggression to show them that he had the advantage, and that they had none. "Be my guess," he said to the first of the five men, "you think you're going to get out of here in a short time. It ain't gonna happen. The bought and paid for judge has disappeared, and all the rest of the judges in this jurisdiction are reluctant to let any of you walk easily."

"Don't matter," the man snarled back. "They'll be gettin' me out plenty quick."

"What they are that?"

"Too damn bad for you if you don't know. They got more power than what you could ever imagine, let alone have."

Mack smiled at the man. "You're living in a dream world. You're going to be locked up for a good long time. When we get through with our investigation, there's no doubt that we'll have proof that all of you are connected with several kidnappings, rapes, and murders. That will keep you in prison for life."

"I ain't never done nothing like that."

"The fact is, you have. What you were trying to do when we arrested you is proof enough for us in this office. We also know that you and the people you work for are guilty of multiple accounts of kidnapping when you've assisted in forcing people into nursing homes, and that you're also involved in human trafficking. Particularly kidnapping young girls and selling them into slavery to be used as prostitutes. That's Darrin Whitcomb's specialty, and it goes way beyond simple kidnapping. It includes multiple counts of murder."

"I don't care what any of that stuff includes. There ain't no way you can prove I done any of them things."

Mack continued his questioning for a while, but ended it without any positive result. It wasn't until he questioned the fourth man that he got anything of value. The man gave him the location of one of Darrin's hideouts.

Before Mack continued the questioning of the men, he informed Lisa. They put together the deputies needed to raid the place. As was the other place of Darren's they raided, this one was also deep in the woods off an old country road.

Unfortunately, when they got there, it was empty, and it was obvious that Darrin wasn't coming back. After the failure of the raid on Darrin's hideout, Mack turned over the rest of the questioning to Paul Danielson. He had the most experience when it came to questioning criminals, so Mack hoped he would get better results. Doing so, also allowed him to get back out in the community and do what he did best. Work within the local people, solving day to day problems as they occurred, along with trying to make it a better place to live.

One of the things he'd done was assist the school system with teaching children of all ages about the environment and the importance of caring for it. Along with the standard methods of teaching them, involving them in the community garden he created had proved to be an excellent teaching tool. As the children involved learned the difference between organic and chemical gardening, they also learned that about farming and all aspects of the right and wrong way of lifestyles in general.

Because of the success with that project, and because he believed that if a child was going to truly understand nature, the child should get out in nature, he pushed ahead to organize classes to be held in the refuge.

He was sure that explaining the recovery happening there after the fire, would be a great illustration of nature itself at work. It would also provide a platform to explain why, as disastrous as the fire was, it wasn't as bad as cutting it all down would have been. The damage done by cutting down a forest went far deeper than fire did.

And finally, it was the best way to point out how the claims the refuge was dead, made by politicians and corporate people whose goal it was to totally destroy the refuge for their own monetary gain, were totally wrong.

As each group of children first arrived at the refuge, they were shocked at the obvious destruction. That impression made them question the reasons for being there.

That quickly changed as they slowly walked the trails and their teachers pointed out the various ways so much of the refuge was already coming back to life. Long before the tour was over, all the children, regardless of age, were impressed by the resilience of nature.

Mack was only occasionally able to attend the classes, but when he did, it was with great deal of satisfaction. He knew it was, in the scheme of things, a small happening. Even so, it was a start toward changing how people saw the environment. And if the environment, along with it the human race, were going to be saved they needed to start somewhere.

CHAPTER 28

One of the things Lisa requested when she got out of the hospital was a new vehicle. A new pickup equipped the same as Mack's, to be exact. Since the county wasn't about to provide it, she and Mack did. The cost never concerned either one of them, and they justified spending the money on Lisa because they knew it would improve her ability to do her job. That went a long way to alleviate some of the guilt Lisa felt about spending so much money on herself.

The day the dealer called to tell her the truck was ready, Mack was patrolling out in the far reaches of the county, so she asked one of the deputies in the office to take her there.

As it always does, it took some extra time, for paper signing and other tasks, at the dealers. So, Lisa sent the deputy back to the office. When she left the dealer in her new pickup, it proved to be too much temptation for her. She couldn't bring herself to go directly back to the office. She simply had to take the truck for a ride.

In her excitement about her new truck, she forgot to pay as much attention as she should have to her surroundings. She was out of town, on a county road with no other traffic when she realized she was being tailed. Since she could see in her mirrors that there were at least two men in the large sedan following her, she should have been scared. Or at least concerned.

Instead, she was angry. All she wanted to do was take a ride in her new truck, to see how it felt driving it. So now here come some probable hired enforcers tailing her. Most likely sent by Heavenly Homes. Her only thoughts about that were, "Enough is enough. If you people want to play games with me, then we damn well will play games."

She continued on the county road, knowing that less than two miles down the road, an old township road traveled off to the right. The road was only lightly maintained and was made more of loose sand than gravel. Much of it also curved around and through ponds and wetlands.

As soon as she turned onto the road, she put the truck into four-wheel drive, giving herself a definite advantage over the car behind her. She also had the same advantage Wanda had when she was chased. She knew the road far better than the driver behind her.

It quickly became a no contest, as she easily outpaced those tailing her. Unlike Wanda though, she was downright angry, and thoroughly tired of having her life screwed up by nasty little criminals. This time she was going to do something about it.

When she came to a small meadow, she used it to turn around, then kicked up the speed of her pickup as she headed back toward the car which was following her. When she came in sight of it, her high speed shocked the car's driver. At first he froze, not turning or slowing down. Before he could think about it, she was nearly on top of them. Suddenly there was nothing he could do other than try to get the hell out of the way in order to avoid the inevitable head-on crash. He turned sharply to his right as he accelerated to get out of her way.

He did, but only by inches. Unfortunately for him, and the other three men in the car, his turn sent him flying into a rather deep pond. His original speed, along with his last-minute acceleration, carried him out far enough to land in the deep water of the pond.

Because the men in the car considered themselves to be truly macho males, none of them were wearing seat belts. Between the sharp turn the car made, along with hitting the water hard, the men were seriously shaken up. Being totally unprepared for what happened, the two in the back were especially slammed around hard. It was enough to knock them both unconscious. They didn't make it out of the car.

The other two men surfaced at about the same time. They didn't do anything aggressive until they were safely up on the road. Even though Lisa was pointing her gun at them, they were still sure a female as small as her couldn't possibly harm them.

They were from somewhere a far distance from Clayborne County and the state of Minnesota, or they would have known better. Instead, all they knew was that she was the acting sheriff and needed constant protection by her deputies. Now there were no deputies. They both drew their weapons with the intent of killing her. That's what they were being paid for.

Lisa, on the other hand, was rated expert on the firing range, and had been hardened enough by life so she had no hesitation when it came to pulling the trigger on the powerful weapon in her hand. And at the close range she would be shooting, the likelihood of her hitting either one of them in a less that lethal spot was highly unlikely.

"Don't be stupid," she told them as they raised their weapons.

They didn't listen, so she fired a quick warning shot. They ignored it, thinking she just missed them. They continued to raise their guns, the man who'd been driving the car moving slightly slower than the other man.

Seeing that, Lisa took out the faster of the two men. Her single shot at him shattered his heart. She swung her gun in the direction of the driver of the car. He quickly fired at her, but was wide of the mark. She returned fire and didn't miss. His mouth dropped open in surprise as the bullet invaded his chest. Then he dropped to the ground where he died.

Lisa took a deep breath, then let out a long sigh of disgust. She stood there, looking at the two bodies. She knew she was supposed to feel bad about what she'd just done, but she couldn't make herself do it. She'd had too many run-ins with those kinds of men to have any feelings about them, other than the relief that came from knowing they weren't ever again going to hurt anyone else.

She put in all the calls for the needed backup and waited. She wasn't worried about anyone trying to prove she'd done anything wrong. The evidence around her was proof enough for her case of self-defense. Especially since the one man did shoot at her.

All of that being true, she was still sure she was in for some serious scolding when Mack got there. He wasn't going to be at all pleased that she'd driven off on her own the way she did. She knew he was right too. So, she wasn't going to be able to defend herself much when he did get after her.

Most of the support people were already there when he arrived. The look on his face went beyond serious when he got out of his pickup. It told her that he was probably very upset with her.

But he first talked to Paul Danielson, then one of the other deputies. The wrecker arrived to pull the car out of the pond while he talked, so he watched the two men who came with it as they worked. One of the men took off his shirt and shoes, then dove into the water to check out the car. He confirmed that there were two bodies still in it.

As they prepared the rigging, they'd need to hoist the car out of the water, Mack finally joined her. He knew she was worried about what he was going to say. That was, in his opinion, exactly as it should be. Especially since she'd promised not to go out on her own the way she did.

The problem he had though, was the fact that he really wasn't angry. It was definitely true that she shouldn't have done it, it was also true that if was him in her shoes, the odds were that he would have done the same thing. So he decided he wasn't going to give her any hell. He was only asking her not to do it again.

To let her know immediately that everything was okay between them, he took her in his arms and kissed her like he meant it. When he pulled away from her, the look on her face was shock.

"Please," he said, "just tell me you won't do this again.'

Tears filled her eyes while a smile filled her face before she answered. "No, Mack, I won't."

He nodded okay, then went back to see if he could assist the men working with the wrecker.

CHAPTER 29

Dell Whitcomb was finding it near impossible to believe. Four professional killers bested by one small female. Not only where they beaten, they were now dead. They were supposed to be the best management could provide. And she didn't have so much as a scratch on her. Initially, all they were supposed to do was watch the sheriff's and her deputy husband's activities, until they found the opportunity to kill them both.

What they were supposed to do, however, and what they did, weren't the same thing. So once again, the company lost four much needed men, and the sheriff and the family she married into were still in control.

Given the fact that going after any of them directly wasn't proving to be at all fruitful, he mulled over other possibilities. There weren't many, he realized, and only one he was somewhat sure could give him some leverage. So, he began his planning for his attack on what he perceived as an opening he could use against Sheriff Lisa Thomas.

As he did, Lisa was becoming ever more restless. She was careful to follow Mack's request, and to always be sure to have someone along with her when she left the office. Even then, she never went farther than to a local cafe to eat, or a local business for other necessities. And as much as she wanted to drive her new truck, she still rode to and from the sheriff's office with Mack.

Putting up with those restrictions was something she could deal with, even though she definitely didn't like them. But the restrictions on her personal life were wearing heavily on her. Especially not being able to visit her own family. She dearly missed her younger sister and brother, her father, and equally as much her father's wife.

After the death of his first wife, he remarried a woman who proved to be a near perfect partner on his dairy farm, a wonderful mother to his two younger children, and a good friend to Lisa.

So, on their way home one evening, she finally told Mack. He wasn't surprised by what she said, only surprised when she did that it had taken her so long to do so.

"All you needed to do, Lisa," he said, "was to tell me you wanted to go see them. When do you want to go? Right Now? Or maybe later tonight or tomorrow?"

"Let's go home, so I can take a shower and get out of this uniform. That'll give them time to get the evening milking done too."

"Good idea. If we go while they're still milking, we won't get much chance to visit."

When they got to the farm, Bob Anderson and his wife Beth were just leaving the milk room attached to the barn. That meant that the last of the evening chores (cleaning the miking equipment) was done, and they'd be free to visit.

After their initial greetings, Bob and Beth excused themselves to shower and change clothes. With that task completed, the four of them decided to go out to eat. The other two children had already eaten and were old enough now to stay home on their own.

They went to a local bar called the Mystic Curve Inn to eat. It only served basic hamburgers, fries, a few sandwiches, and salad. As always, Mack ordered a bacon cheeseburger, fries, and a small salad. The burger and fries had always been what he ordered when he ate out. The salad was added after he married Lisa. It was one of the very few things she insisted he do.

They managed to spend a very pleasant evening together, but ended it early because of the early hours a dairy farm required. They'd driven in separate vehicles to the bar, so they said their goodnights there.

Bob and Beth got in the pickup first. Mack took a moment to kiss his wife before they got into his pickup. As they did, she noticed a dark sedan that was parked along the side of the road pull out as Bob and Beth drove by. She pointed it out to Mack.

"I don't like that," he said. "I don't like that at all." He knew that if the sedan was following Bob and Beth, he could stay a farther distance behind it than he normally would in this situation. He knew where they were going if they were following, and they were.

When they reached the farm, the car stopped until Bob and Beth were out of their pickup, then drove away. Since they hadn't committed any crime, there was nothing Mack and Lisa could do to them, so they let them go. Instead, they stopped to talk to Bob and Beth, who were surprised to see them.

"What are you doing back here?" Bob asked. "I thought you were going home."

"That was the plan," Mack said.

"Until you got followed home," Lisa added.

"Are you sure?" Bob asked.

"There's no doubt about it," Mack told him. "And that's bad news. It means you and your family are now a target."

"Why would we be anyone's target? We haven't done anything to anyone."

"No, Dad," Lisa said, "but we have. They've been coming after us for quite a while. We've stopped them every time. Often enough, I think, so they're getting desperate. I could be wrong, but they might go after you to get to me."

"That sure doesn't sound good at all. What do you suggest we do about it? It's not like we can run and hide. Not with near a hundred cows to milk twice a day. And the kids still have to go to school."

"We realize that," Mack said. "The only solution is to give you protection. We'll need to keep a deputy posted here around the clock."

"The trouble with that, Mack, is the county isn't going to want to pay for it. If I even ask, you know what they'll claim."

"I know. All the usual bullshit about how the county can't afford it, and that you are favoring your family. So, we aren't going to ask the county. We'll hire the deputies as private citizens and pay them at a rate of time and a half their regular pay, since the hours they put in would be overtime if the county was paying them."

"I don't know if I can let you do that," Bob argued. "That would cost you guys a lot of money."

"Not enough to matter, Dad," Lisa explained. "There's no amount of money worth more than you, Beth, and the kids.

"And I totally agree with that, Bob," Mack added.

"Does that mean we'll have someone in the house or the barn all the time?" Beth asked. "That could get old in a hurry."

"No," Mack answered. "The deputy who's on duty will remain in their car or outside. They'll be better able to keep watch from there than inside the house or barn. They're all well trained enough to know that on that kind of assignment, your protection is their first and only duty."

"When are they going to start?"

"First thing in the morning."

"What about tonight?"

"That'll be my job," Mack told them. "I'll be here until I get relieved in the morning."

"What about Lisa?" Bob asked. "Didn't you say, earlier tonight, that you weren't going to let her be alone until you catch the man after her?"

"I did, and I'm not going to. After you and Beth get settled in for the night, we'll call a deputy to come and take her home. She'll also be picked up by a deputy in the morning, to give her a ride to the office."

"You're going to get awful tired before morning," Beth said. "How are you going to manage to stay awake all night?"

"To start with, I was hoping you owned a thermos you could fill up with coffee for me. That'd help a lot."

"I can do that," Beth said, smiling slightly. Their conversation had served as a reminder of her past relationship with Mack. They'd been lovers for a long time before she split up with him because of the relationship that developed between her and Bob. It was a past they both remembered fondly, and with absolutely no regrets. In fact, when she was reminded of it, it still gave her a slight tingling sensation she never got from anything else.

Bob was in bed and Lisa had left for home when she brought Mack his coffee. She lingered a moment after handing it to him. They were both filled with past memories and previously buried desires when she moved closer.

She looked up and into his eyes. "I know," she said, "that we will never do anything about what we're both feeling. But if things were even slightly different in the lives, we've both chosen, I'd make love to you in a minute."

With that, she wrapped her hand around his neck, pulled his head down and kissed him like she meant it. She was halfway between a smile and tears when they broke it. She shook her head slightly, turned, and walked away. He watched her until she went inside and closed the door behind her. It proved to be a long night for Mack.

CHAPTER 30

"They'll be easy to grab," the dark-haired man said. "We'll do it when they get off the school bus."

"What about the deputy?" Dell asked. "What will you do if he sees you and gets involved?"

"Whatever it takes," he answered.

"You'd be okay with killing a sheriff's deputy?"

"I don't see why not. One dead body's the same as another as far as I'm concerned."

"Well, good. Because if this goes the same as everything else we've tried, it's entirely possible you'll have to. So, are you ready to do it?"

"Yup. The plan is tomorrow afternoon. The thing is, there's something else I want besides the money."

"Really? And what might that be?"

"The girl. I ain't had one that young for way too long, and since we're grabbing her anyway, I want a piece of her."

"Fine by me. Just don't rough her up too much. She'll bring a good price when we sell her, if she's still in decent shape."

"We'll just have to see how that goes, Dell. It'll mostly depend on how she reacts. I'll only get as rough as necessary."

His car was parked behind some trees, just slightly off the road and a short distance from the driveway when the bus arrived. His partner was in the driver's seat, his hands on the wheel and the motor running. He was even closer, waiting behind a giant old oak, sure no one could see him. His plan was to take only the girl, believing she'd be enough to force the sheriff to tow the line.

There proved to be a serious flaw in his plan, however. As they walked up the driveway, the boy, Ricky, walked close to his sister, Julie. He was also on the same side of her as the man waiting. That gave the man only seconds to make a decision. He decided to go after the boy. A kid was a kid after all. And since he was the sheriff's younger brother, he should serve as nearly as good a bait as the girl.

It was a serious mistake. Ricky was tall, with longer than normal arms, and was far more alert than he appeared. He picked up on the man as soon as he moved. Ricky pushed his sister, Julie, out of the way and at the same time stretched out his long arm to block the man. His open hand landed in his face, momentarily blocking the man's view.

"Run, Julie," he yelled at the top of his lungs.

She screamed as she regained her balance and took off running. This left the man no choice but to cut and run. The deputy on duty, now alerted, drew his gun, searched out the man, took aim, and fired. His first shot was near miss, but his second, although rather low, did a lot of damage to the man's posterior. He was bleeding heavily as he jumped into the waiting car.

The deputy managed a couple more shots at the fleeing car, but wasn't sure if he hit it or not. He was filled with frustration as he walked back to check on the kids.

He found the whole family together. The parents, Bob and Beth, watched him approach, both of them with a serious look of concern. Julie had her arms around her brother, holding on tight. The look on her face said it all. He was her hero now. Their relationship in the past had always been a typical teenage brother and sister one. All that changed when his outstretched hand blocked their would-be attacker.

Even though Ricky's reactions were mostly instinctive, she knew that he'd stopped the man from having any chance of taking her. For that. she'd be forever grateful to her brother.

For him, the way she was hanging on to him was more embarrassing than anything. Even so, he did nothing to stop her. Young as he was, he was still smart enough to know she needed the calming influence it gave her. So, she was still holding on to him when Lisa and Mack arrived.

They were both visibly upset when they got out of Mack's pickup. For Lisa, it was mostly concern for her family. Mack was simply furious. His anger eased very little as the deputy explained what happened.

"You handled it the way you should have," Mack told him when he completed the explanation.

"The thing is," the deputy answered, "it's the kid, Ricky, who deserves any credit for running those guys off. It took guts to take care of his sister first, then stop the guy before he did anything to save himself."

When Lisa heard that, she couldn't help herself. She moved to Ricky's side, opposite the one Julie was hanging onto, and gave her brother a huge hug. It was enough to make him blush. Hugs from sisters wasn't something he was used to. Embarrassed or not though, he couldn't help but smile.

Mack was anxious to begin a search for the wounded man, so when it seemed as though everyone had settled down, he asked Lisa, "Are you ready to go? There's still a chance we'll find the one with a bullet in him."

"I think I'll stay here for a while, Mack. Just in case those men are stupid enough to come back for a second try. You can pick me up later."

"That makes sense," Mack agreed, kissed her goodbye, and left.

Since there was so little doubt in his mind about who was behind the incident, he decided to check out Heavenly Homes first. Since he didn't have a search warrant, he just did a quick walk through most of the building. The few people he stopped to question denied seeing anyone who appeared to be hurt.

He checked the hospital next. There'd been no one at the emergency room with a gunshot wound. By then, it was getting late and he was ready to call it a day.

Lisa was waiting for him in the house when he got back to the farm. She left the couch when he went into the living room and greeted him with a hug and kiss. Beth watched from the chair she was in, with a face lacking any expression. It wasn't until Mack caught her eye that he noticed what she was feeling.

The look in them was one of something more than friendship, but also something lost. He remembered the kiss she gave him and shivered. It was strong enough for Lisa to feel. She backed away from him.

"What is it, Mack?" she asked, her eyes searching his face. "What's wrong."

"It's not something I can explain," he said. "It was just a feeling I had." He looked again at Beth, but she averted her eyes.

Lisa hugged him again. He took a deep breath and tried hard to push the memories now flooding him, of Beth especially, but also all the other woman who'd been part of his life. He looked at Lisa, and was as thankful as a person could be thankful, for having her in his life.

Whatever had been between him, and Beth was gone now, and no matter what, it was something they'd never get back. He caught Beth's eyes again, and they told him the same thing he'd just felt. Even so, somewhere inside a small part of each of them still held a soft spot for the other.

Knowing that, Mack tried to turn his thoughts to other things as he and Lisa drove home. Unfortunately, she didn't let him.

"Do you and Beth still have some feelings for each other?" she bluntly asked.

"What the hell brought that on?" Mack asked, surprised at her question.

"The look in her eyes and that shiver I felt when it was there. It seemed as though she was having some kind of an effect on you. It went passed just a simple friendship.'

"I could tell you lies and deny that there was anything there. But I won't. Before I say anything more though, I have to tell you that I love you, and you are the one and only women that I want in my life. No one and nothing will ever change that."

"Is that your way of telling me there is something between you two?"

"Sort of. But what's there is something of the past and still in the past. I have fond memories of our relationship, and I guess she does too. But neither one of us had any intention at all of taking that beyond the memory stage. She loves your dad and I love you. It stops there."

"I hope so, Mack. It would hurt my dad a lot if it was something else."

"What about you. You almost sound like it wouldn't matter that much to you."

"It would. More than I think you'd believe."

"I believe it. It would be more than I could handle if I lost you. So, you can believe that I'd never do anything to would make me lose you."

"Good," she said, "and don't ever forget that. Life's too damn short to mess it up for something that isn't worth it."

She kissed him on the cheek, leaned back against the seat, and smiled. He breathed a sigh of relief.

CHAPTER 31

Darrin Whitcomb was enjoying himself. He felt secure in his new residence, two counties away from Clayborne County. It was located in a sparsely populated rural area, and the old farmstead was set back a good distance from the gravel road it was on.

Along with the house, which was definitely livable, there were several outbuildings. Among them were a barn, still watertight, and a large chicken coop. The coop was once used as a small hatchery, so it was insulated and had an operable furnace. That made it a great place to hold the girls he and others of his far-reaching group kidnapped to sell to the dealers in trafficked women on the east coast.

He was just two women away from a full order and planning to grab another one shortly. With that done, he was determined to take the one he considered to be first prize of any of or all of the females he could ever force into the life of prostitution. Something all the women he dealt with were doomed to. Forcing Lisa Thomas into that life wasn't just a goal for him. It was an obsession. He couldn't see how he could ever be satisfied until he got his revenge and satiated his hatred.

Killing her wasn't enough punishment for her. He needed to know that she'd be suffering. Not just for years either. For the rest of her life. Anything less, and he would never be satisfied.

He knew that accomplishing his task was going to be extremely difficult. So difficult, that it would be impossible for a lessor man. But because he considered himself to be superior to nearly everyone, he was sure he could not fail.

He knew that he needed to carefully plan it, to the point he'd memorized every step he'd take to fulfill his mission. So now he started what he considered would be the most satisfying thing he ever did. Lisa Thomas would be his in every way possible, right up to the moment he sold her into the world of prostitution. Those thoughts not only excited him, they also filled him with a restless anticipation he found hard to contain.

Containing her restlessness was also a problem bugging Lisa. Her's wasn't as bad as Darrin's, but it was becoming serious, nonetheless. Given the constant threat to her with Darrin Whitcomb still out there and free to move as he chose, she felt as if she was never alone. It was suffocating her.

The sorry truth was, other than using the bathroom, she never really was alone. Her constant edginess was reaching the point that it was frustrating not only Mack, but her coworkers too. Mack finally decided he needed to do something about it.

"I think," he told her on their way home about midweek, "that you and I are going to go out dancing on Saturday night. That is, if you'd like too."

"I can't think of anything I'd like better, Mack. I know I've been a real pain in the butt lately, but being watched and having everything I do controlled constantly has been incredibly frustrating. Being able to go out and kick up my heals some would be a pure blessing."

Mack was pleased with himself when she reacted the way she did. He'd been hoping she would. Both for her sake, and the sake of those around her. So, he vowed to make it a late night as well as a good night.

Given how excited she was about the idea of the two of them having a night out, she surprised him the next morning at breakfast. She did it right after they got to Ben and Theresa's.

"Mack and I are going out Saturday night," she announced. "We're going out for dinner, and then dancing. We'd love it if all of you came with us." She paused, smiled, and continued. "we'd especially like to have you come, Sue," she said directly to Sue, who was there for breakfast, as she almost always was.

At first there was a stunned silence from everyone, Sue included. Not because they didn't want to join Lisa and Mack on their night out. Instead, it was because they were surprised, after what she'd been going through, she would ask them along. They all would have expected her to want to be alone with Mack.

"Well, how about it?" Lisa asked, herself surprised she didn't get an immediate answer.

Even Mack was confused. Not only from Lisa's request, but from his family's lack of an answer. Quickly though, as he usually did, Roy was the first to respond.

"I can't think of anything, Lisa, any of us would rather do than go out for a good time with you two. The thing is, after the way things have been going, are you sure you really want us too."

"Well hell yes I want you too." Lisa said, a broad smile now on her face. "If for no other reason, Roy, so I can dance with you." With that, she gave Wanda a wink.

It was returned, but Wanda also asked, "Are you guys sure this is a good idea. You still have those people out there hoping to kill the both of you."

"I have to admit," Mack answered, "I was a little concerned about it to start. But not if you guys all come along. I doubt like hell than anyone is going to want to screw around with us when we're together. And even if they did, I'm confident we can handle it."

"I think you're right," Roy said. "Anyone screws with us, isn't going to like how we deal with it."

"I can second that," Ben agreed. "There's not a one of us here who isn't damn sick and tired of useless criminals messing with our lives. There's been days lately, when I've almost wished the latest of them would try something, just so we could teach them something about right and wrong."

Theresa couldn't help herself. She laughed. "Ben's right, you know. It would be a fine thing to teach those people a lesson or two."

"I agree with all of that," Wanda said. "Even so, my gut tells me that we'd better be damn careful anyway. There's still some very bad people out there."

As the breakfast progressed, the three women of the group moved the conversation from things they were concerned about to plans for the night. Choosing a place was easy. The Mystic Curve Inn always had live music on Saturday nights, which played mostly country. Since that was everyone's favorite, there wasn't anywhere else anyone wanted to go.

None of them were concerned about the food. The menu was short and simple, but what was on it was always good, and served in generous portions.

The last thing they talked about was what to wear. For the three men, it was simple. Blue Jeans, a western cut shirt, and cowboy boots. Theresa and Wanda talked about various dresses, but Lisa stayed undecided. She was most often more comfortable in an outfit similar to what the men would wear, but also thought she owed it to Mack to wear something more feminine.

She still hadn't made a decision when they left for work. In fact, she didn't make that decision until she was getting ready to go out Saturday night. She first dressed in jeans and a somewhat tight blouse. Even though the jeans were tight enough to show off her near perfect figure, she decided it was sexy enough, but didn't quite give her look she wanted to show Mack. It took her five tries before the black skirt she put on gave her the look she really wanted to portray. Its length was modest enough while still managing to show off a decent amount of her perfect legs. When she joined Mack, his grin told her she'd made the right choice.

Each of the couples decided to drive, so if anyone got tired and wanted to leave, the rest could stay. Sue rode with Roy and Wanda. Mack and Lisa were particularly pleased with that decision, since they planned to make a late night out of it. They knew doing so would be good for Lisa. She needed to burn off a lot of excess energy if she was going to shed herself of the pent-up frustration her life had lately filled her with.

They arrived at the bar early, so they could find a table large enough for all of them. The women drank wine with the meal, and the men shared a pitcher of beer. They all managed to relax, so the conversation was light, and filled with talk of vegetable growing, raising cattle. and being an inexperienced CEO of a growing corporation.

The last part of the conversation was dominated by Wanda, since she was that CEO. After some discussion, she said what she'd been wanting to say for a while. "I've appreciated the confidence all of you've had in me." She paused, hoping she didn't upset anyone with what else she had to say. "But to tell you all the truth, what I'd really like best about the job is to leave it. I think the company is getting too big for me to want to continue to be part of it. I've always been somewhat of a country girl. Since

I've been married to Roy, I've become a total country girl."

Everyone was somewhat surprised by her comments, except Mack. "I completely understand how you feel, Wanda," he said. "I also think we all feel at least somewhat that way about the company. Since we've all gotten most of what we put in it to start it, I think it's time we turned it over to someone, or some company, who can manage it in a way that it will keep on growing. We just have to make sure they'll continue to operate it on the principles it was founded on."

To no one's surprise, there were six heads shaking yes in agreement with him. It only took a little more discussion to reach the agreement that finding that person or company would now be a priority.

Shortly after that decision, the music started. Rather than country, the first song was a fast, old-time rock and roll. Lisa did the unexpected then, and grabbed Roy's hand to accompany her to the dance floor. It was a good choice, Roy being more capable on the dance floor than Mack was. Especially when it was rock and roll.

She made up for it though, when they played the first slow song. She returned to the table and got Mack. Out on the dance floor, she kissed him with the kind of passion strong enough to make him wish he could take her home right then. He couldn't, but he got the next best thing when she held him tight enough to tell him she belonged to him, and only him.

As the night progressed, they changed partners frequently on the dance floor. The three men were kept busy dancing nearly every song, while one of the four women sat out each song.

Lisa used the rest room when the band took their break after the first set. Wanda went with her. She didn't go again until the middle of the third set. She was dancing with Ben until he excused himself to use the restroom.

Lisa didn't decide she needed to use the women's until Ben was already on his way back. They missed each other as she went into the hallway going to it. Someone had turned out the light in the women's room when she opened the door. She found it strange, because it was something that normally wasn't done, but went in anyway.

The blow she receives to the back of her head as she did, knocked her senseless. Darrin Whitcomb couldn't believe his good luck. He never would have imagined he'd be so lucky. Here he was, finally out for a good time with his brother, and the very people he was hunting show up. He was full of smiles as he dragged her out the little used back door of the bar.

He got lucky a second time when he got Lisa out the door before anyone came down the hall to use a restroom. From there, he carried her to his car, Zip tied her hands behind her and her legs together. He threw her on the floor in back, and quickly left the place. His destination was his new headquarters where he kept his captive girls.

And ultimately, the total rape of Lisa Thomas. Something, he was totally confident that no one could stop.

CHAPTER 32

Dell was having too good a time with the ladies sitting with him at his table, to even noticed Darrin was missing. It took about the same amount of time before anyone realized Lisa was missing. Because of the way they'd been changing partners on the dance floor, everyone kept thinking she was out dancing with someone else.

It wasn't until all six of them sat down at their table that it hit them. Their initial search for her was frantic, and when there was no sign of her, they were close to panic.

It was worse for Mack than anyone else. Not only because she was his wife who he loved with all his heart, but just as much because it brought up memories of a woman he'd been engaged to years before. She was in danger at the time, and even though it worried him to no end, he'd given in to her wishes. She went to work on her own, where she was murdered one evening after work. That memory doubled his concern for Lisa.

They were all on their second search through the bar when Roy spotted Dell Whitcomb. He was sitting with a small group of people. Because of his position at their table, only his back was facing the rest of the bar. They hadn't noticed him during the first search, but Roy recognized him this time. He called Mack over and they approached him together, each stopping on either side of him.

Roy was the first to speak. "One question," he said, "where's your brother."

Before Dell could answer, a young lady who'd had too much to drink, answered, "He left already."

Dell glared at her. "He wasn't bothering anyone, and he was only here for a while." It was the only answer he could give, because he didn't know what Darrin might have done, nor did he know yet that Lisa was missing.

Roy grabbed his shoulder, forcing Dell to face him. "Are you sure about that?" His powerful hand squeezed his shoulder hard enough to make Dell wince.

He tried to pull away from Roy. "What the hell, Man? What's with you? What is it you want?"

"I want to know where your brother is. Now! Lisa Thomas is missing, and we think he has her."

"None of us here have the slightest idea where he is," Dell answered. He kept his voice at an even level, knowing from the look on Roy's face that it would be best not to piss him off any farther.

"But he was here?"

"Yeah, he was. He just took off without saying he was leaving. I have no idea where he went or why."

But he now did know now why Darrin left. He got Lisa.

That was all Mack and Roy needed to hear. They had little doubt about what happened to Lisa. That knowledge filled Mack with the worst kind of dread. Was this going to be Mandy all over again. If it was, he wasn't sure he could handle it this time.

As bad as it was for him, he managed to pull himself together enough to confront Dell Whitcomb. "If anything happens to her," he threatened, "you and your brother are going to pay for it. And pay dearly."

"You can't threaten me that way," Dell complained. "I haven't done anything wrong."

"Bullshit!" Mack spit back at him. "You've done enough wrong to deserve a lifetime prison sentence ten times over. And if something happens to Lisa, what you get from me will be much worse than that could possibly be."

Roy moved in on them. "Where does he live?" he demanded to know.

"I don't know."

"How about I break your nose to start? Think that might jog your memory some?"

"You can't do that. I'll have you arrested."

"I can and will." he grabbed Dell's shirt, lifted him up off his chair, and moved his right arm back, as if he was ready to swing it. "It's up to you," he said.

Being the coward he was, he told Roy about the place Darrin was staying. The place he described was the deserted one they already raided. Had he been a normal human, Dell might have felt guilty about telling the lie. But he was a long way from normal.

His only hope was that Darrin would kill Lisa before anyone caught up with him. Doing so would be a good start as far as Dell was concerned.

But Darrin had no intention of killing Lisa. She was still young enough to be acceptable to the men out east that he dealt with. Even better, she was as beautiful a woman as he'd ever be able to provide. Beautiful enough, he thought, to bring him a premium price. There were a lot of bodies for sale out there in the human marketplace, but any with her beauty were very rare.

But rare or not, it was his full intention to have his way with her in every way possible. Doing so might lower her market value, but the satisfaction of doing everything possible to her was, for him, worth more than money. He also didn't care that much if she didn't wake up before he did her. It was the doing that thrilled him the most, not her response. Either way, there was nothing to stop him now.

And that was something she was beginning to realize too, as she slowly regained consciousness. Her hands were tightly bound by the plastic zip ties, and so were her legs. She knew she was in deep trouble. She could tell she was in a moving vehicle, and because she was, there was virtually no chance anyone could come to her rescue.

She also had little doubt about what whoever had kidnapped her intended to do to her. This was her second time in this situation, and she dreaded the outcome. The first time it happened she'd been raped countless times and expected the same thing would happen this time. If only she had some kind of weapon, some way to defend herself.

She did her best to fight the ties, but quickly knew it was a losing proposition. Soon after she realized that, the vehicle she was in stopped. The driver of the car got out, then opened the back door. Darrin Whitcomb leered at her, gave her an evil grin, then lifted her off the car's floor.

As shaken as she was with the knowledge of who had taken her, she was also perversely relieved of the pressure from the small lump on the floor of the car. It was a painful irritation bothering her since she woke up.

Darrin only had one thing on his mind when he carried her through the door of the old farmhouse. And that was what he planned to do to her. In his haste, he laid her down on the floor in the living room rather than carry her into his bedroom. Even in the incredible fear she felt, she was irritated again with the lump under her back. "Where the hell was it coming from?" she wondered. Having something stuck to the outside of her skirt seemed highly unlikely.

While he ripped open her blouse and tore off her bra, she moved her hands just enough to find the lump. When she did, she felt a thrill run through her. The lump was inside the waist band of her skirt. She was wearing the skirt she wore when she'd captured the three murderers not long after the refuge fire. Taking the knife out of the skirts waistband was something she'd forgotten to do when she put the skirt away. What she remembered was how to take it out now, and how to put it to good use.

As Darrin struggled with his pants, she was no longer afraid of what he might do. Instead, she was happy she'd spent so much time practicing the moves she needed to remove the knife/lump from her waist band, which was actually a retractable switch blade knife. A knife with a three inch, surgically sharp, blade.

Once he had his pants down around his knees, Darrin went after her panties. By then, she had the knife out and the ties on her wrists cut. He was struggling with her so hard, he didn't notice what she was doing. In fact, he still hadn't noticed that she was awake. That meant she could ease her right hand, holding the knife, out from under her back and to her side.

When he thought he'd gotten her panties far enough out of the way, he slid up between her legs and set himself in position to push inside her. She didn't hesitate. With perfect accuracy, the swing of her right hand sent the knife blade slashing across his face. At eye level. It entered his eyes very quickly, slicing them deep, one at a time.

Darrin didn't realize what happened until the pain hit him. He tried to hold onto the source of the pain, only to discover that he was now totally blind. He screamed and fumbled around trying to find her throat. He was too slow, and she managed to slash both his upper arms with another swing of the knife. She followed it with a push hard enough to get out from under him. Before he could respond to her moves, she cut him again, across his face one more time.

She now had time to cut the ties around her ankles and pull up her panties. With the ability to use her legs properly, she kicked the sitting Darrin with everything she had. Her foot landed under his chin, snapping his head back hard. He dropped to the floor. He was out, if not permanently, at least for a good long time.

As she looked for a phone of some kind to call Mack, she heard someone come in the backdoor of the house. Whoever it was, she knew it was bad. All she had to defend herself was the knife, and she was fairly sure the person coming in would be armed.

She pushed her back against the wall next to the door of the room the sounds were coming from. The person who opened the door came into the room and saw Darrin lying there, he stopped as his mouth dropped open. He then reached for the gun tucked into his belt.

Lisa didn't wait to discuss what happened to Darrin with him. She didn't want to deal with him at all. Instead, with one quick movement, she cut his throat. He dropped his gun, reached for his throat, which was spraying blood out in front of him, made a gurgling sound, fell on the floor and died. She picked up his gun.

Curious now, about where she was and what was going on here, she decided to check it out. She found a dirty kitchen in the room the now dead man came from. Another door leading outdoors was located on the far kitchen wall. She opened it slowly. She could see several buildings, but only one had lights on.

She carefully went out and slowly approached it. Looking in a window, the scene inside horrified her, but didn't surprise her. Four young girls were locked in portable dog kennels. Two men sat at a nearby table playing cards.

Lisa watched through the window for a while, weighing her options. With two men in there, both armed, there was only one choice to make. She knew that none of the normal procedures for this type of situation was going to work.

To start with, she didn't have a phone. She didn't know where she was. And she knew that sooner or later either one or both the men would be looking for the dead man.

She guessed she could try to hide but knew there'd be a good chance they'd find her. If she charged into the building they were in, there'd probably be a gunfight. She could easily lose it, and there was a good chance one or more of the girls could get shot. So again, there was only one option that she could see. So she took it.

She eased open the unlocked door, and as soon she was inside, without the slightest hesitation, shot and killed both men. The girls in the cages were stunned by the shots she fired, but when they saw who they were meant for, they didn't scream in fear.

"It's okay now," Lisa told them. "I'm not here to hurt you. Do any of you know where the keys to the locks on your cages are?"

In unison, the girls said, "On the wall behind you."

Lisa turned around and found several keys hanging from nails. As she opened the cages she asked, "How many men have you girls seen since you've been here?"

"Several," they said. "But only four on a regular basis. One of them isn't here as much, and the other one always here just went into the house. He's really mean, so you better be careful when he comes back out here."

"Don't worry," she explained, "he won't be back."

After she got all the girls free, she brought them into the house where they searched for clothes to wear. She found a cell phone on the dead man in the house and called Mack.

It was an emotional conversation when she told him what happened and apologized for not having the slightest idea where she was.

"If at all possible," Mack told her, "find a vehicle you can use to get you and those girls the hell out of there. Do it as quick as you can. But keep me on the line, so I know what is going on."

Lisa checked Darrin's pockets for his keys. When she didn't find them, she checked the car he was driving. She found them in the ignition. She quickly loaded the girls and drove the hell out of there. Unsure which way to turn at the end of the driveway, she made a right turn. She checked the milage as she drove, giving it to Mack as she drove.

Her turn proved to be the right one, because less than three miles down the dirt road, she came to a two-lane state highway. Again unsure, she turned left this time.

From what little she could see in the moonlight, there was nothing for several miles other than a few farms. From the highway signs she'd seen, she knew she was traveling south, but that was all she knew.

CHAPTER 33

When Lisa's growing frustration was reaching its limits, she finally reached a town. The sign on the side of the road where they entered it said it was Baptism Towers. It was small but did have its own police department. She stopped in front of it, told Mack where she was, and was relieved to find it open and a young cop at the desk inside. She broke her connection with Mack.

"Thank god you're here," she told the cop. "We need your help."

"What kind of help?" he asked, letting his eyes rove over all of her. He smirked as he said, "Someone like you, I'm always glad to help."

"You can get rid of the smirk," she said, letting her instant anger with him show in her voice. "Do you have an adult you can call to assist you. I really do need help, and so do the girls I have with me."

"Really? What girls are those?"

"They are four girls who were kidnapped. We just escaped the place where they were held. Three of the men who were holding them are now dead.

The one still alive isn't likely to be a problem. But it is possible there are more of them. Whoever checks on the place they were, should take plenty of backup with them."

"Really now. A pretty little lady like you is an expert on law enforcement. I think we can handle the situation, whatever it is, without advice from you. Now, I think we should go get them girls you claim to have with you, so's I can decide what to do with the lot of you."

Lisa wasn't feeling right about the way the cop was reacting, so she was thankful she'd tucked the gun she still carried into the back of the waistband of her skirt. She moved her blouse over it as she followed the cop out to the car.

As the girls exited the car, one of them gasped when she saw the cop. "He's one of the men who come around sometimes," she said, her voice a mere whimper.

The cop pulled his gun. "All of you," he snarled, "get the hell into the station." He herded them inside.

There was only one small cell. He forced all of them into it. In his haste to do so, he failed to search any of them. Something he probably wasn't bright enough to do even if he wasn't in a hurry.

Because he'd been working with Darrin Whitcomb for a while now, he didn't consider any of them to be any kind of a threat. He'd had his turn at raping several young women, including two of these, and they hadn't actually given him any kind of problem. So, he was sure none of them would now.

Lisa could see from the look on his face, that he was overconfident. He thought she was just another defenseless girl. For the moment, she was glad he had the attitude he had. She could have easily stopped him at any time, but was now more interested in who else was involved. So, she intended to let things play out for the moment.

She guessed that she should probably be scared, but she was too aggravated and angry. She still had two weapons, between the gun and knife. Mack was on his way, and she was sure, with other people.

The only thing she was missing was the cell phone she took from the dead men. The cop took it away from her right away. He was using it now, trying to call the men Lisa eliminated, and of course, getting no answer. Frustrated, he made a different call.

"Yeah, Chief," he said when he got an answer. "I think it'd be a good idea for you to get over here. We got us a serious situation." He was silent for a moment, then said, "It's those girls. They got away somehow. I've got them all locked up in the cell." He was silent again. Then said, "No, five this time."

He hung up the phone, then walked up to the cell holding Lisa and the girls. He starred at them one at the time. They were all at least very pretty, and one almost as beautiful as Lisa, who was surprised when his eyes lingered on her. The others were still scantily dressed, yet he seemed to prefer her.

After a bit, he smiled at her. "I don't know what we're gonna do with you all," he claimed, looking at Lisa, "but before we do it, you and me are going to have some fun. Of that, there's no doubt."

Lisa had a few answers for him, but held her tongue. She knew that nothing she said would have any effect on him. He was too wrapped up in himself to be insulted. And she considered that men who did what he did to women, meant he like the rest of them, was suffering from his own brand of retardation. An evil version of it, yes. But still a version of a definite mental deficiency.

That seemed to show even more when the man he called arrived. He was the chief of police for the town, so he was in charge of both of the town's deputies.

"Did you call out there?" the chief asked the cop at the desk.

"I've tried four times already. They don't answer. She," he pointed to Lisa, "had one of their cell phones when she came here, but I called one of the other ones."

"So why the hell aren't they answering. Come to think of it, they should be calling to tell us they no longer have the girls. What the hell could have happened to them"

"She," the deputy said, still pointing at Lisa, "said they was dead. Three of them anyway."

"That don't sound right to me.," the chief complained. "How could they be dead. They ain't nothing but women. Those are some damn tough men. There ain't no way none of these little beauties could have done anything to them. So, what the hell's going on?"

"Only thing I can figure," said the deputy, "is maybe they got in some kind of fight."

"I can't see that. What the hell would they fight over?"

"Ain't but one thing I can think of," the deputy again pointed out Lisa, a grin on his face now, "except her."

The chief looked hard at Lisa for the first time. He too, smiled. "Well damn," he said, "if she ain't some real good looker, I don't know what it is. Before we finish this, whatever it is, I believe I'm going to have me some of that."

Lisa, pretending she wasn't paying attention to the two men, was actually listening closely to their words. When she heard the chief's comments about her, comments she'd heard way too often, she found herself wishing he would try. She had her own idea of what some part of him she would have. And the knife in the waistband of her black skirt told her exactly how she would get it. If he made the attempt he threatened, it would be harvest time for her. And when she thought about it, she included the deputy in her plans. All she needed was a chance at them.

When the chief finally stopped starring, he turned to the deputy. "I think," he said, "it'd be a good idea for you to take a run up there and see what happened. When you know, give me a call. We'll decide what to do then."

The deputy left, and the police station was quiet for a while. Because there was only a small cot in the cell, most of the girls sat on the floor. Lisa was one of them.

The chief also sat quietly at the desk nearest the cell. As he did, he continued to stare at Lisa. Without realizing what he was doing, he moved his hand between his legs and started rubbing. When he did become aware what he was doing, he decided that there wasn't much point in waiting. He pulled out his gun as he got up from his chair, unlocked the cell and motioned for Lisa to come out.

"Undress and lay down," he instructed her.

She didn't argue, but knew she couldn't take the skirt off. So, she opened her blouse, removed her bra and panties, then pulled up her skirt. As she laid down on the floor she quickly removed the knife from the skirt's waist band. He was too busy trying to remove his pants to notice.

"Now," he said once his pants were gone, "the fun begins."

And it did, but not for him. He hadn't come close to scaring Lisa. What he did was make her extremely angry. And more than angry, absolutely tired of men who thought the greatest thing they could do was rape her. She waited until he'd moved into the right place for her to show him that he'd made a grave error.

This time she knew exactly what she was going to do, so her aim was perfect when she used the knife on him. The slice it made was next to his body, and his manhood was completely gone. Her follow through slashed opened two deep cuts in his arms. He was so shocked he couldn't respond to her. She scrambled out from under him, let him feel the same kick she'd given Darrin, and put her clothes back in order.

She called Mack again as she let the girls out of the cell. As she talked to him, she spotted the chief's lost manhood on the floor. Without any attempt to hide what she was doing, she walked over and stomped on it hard. Several times.

When the girls saw what she was doing two of them turned their heads away. The other two laughed and said, "Good, that's a damn good thing to do with it."

One of them also said, "If I had shoes on, I'd help with that."

After that, it was a matter of waiting for Mack. Lisa wasn't about to call anyone else before he got there. She wasn't feeling all that trusting of men right then.

When Mack arrived, along with Roy, he called 911 to get an ambulance for the barely alive chief. After a short discussion, they decided to call the county sheriff since they were in Jackstone county, not Clayborne county. Mack is the one who talked to the person on duty at the sheriff's office. She said she'd send the sheriff right away.

Lisa told him the whole story when he got there. He immediately had a female deputy take charge of the four girls.

"So," Sheriff Tod Mcintire said, "you were out with your husband and were kidnapped from the bar you were in? Then the kidnapper hauls you up here, you manage to cut him up like you did to the chief here, then you kill three kidnappers all by yourself. After all that you come here to be kidnapped again? That's a hell of a lot to have happened to such pretty little lady."

"You don't believe me?" Lisa asked.

"It's not that exactly," he said, "but your story is highly unlikely."

"I'm not sure where you're coming from, Sheriff, but wherever it is, I strongly suggest you get your head back on straight."

"Thing is, it's been my experience that when anything like this goes down, it's always some kind of lovers spat. I just don't see you doing what you said you did."

Roy, who'd been quiet the whole time, made a suggestion to the sheriff. "It's like this," he told him, "what she's been trying to tell you is true." Then he surprised the sheriff by telling him who Lisa was.

"You've got to be kidding me," the shocked sheriff said. "She's the Sheriff of Clayborne County? I heard they had a female on the job, but we kind of expected some two hundred pound broad with a face like a blood hound."

"Sorry to disappoint you sheriff, but that's who she is."

"Well then, how did Darrin Whitcomb manage to kidnap her?"

"They've been after Darrin for quite a while," Roy explained, "and the fact he happened to be in that crowded bar at the same time we were is one of those freak things we all dread happening. It was almost as weird as Lisa accidentally wearing the skirt she did."

"Sorry," the sheriff argued, "but the whole story I've heard so far is too far-fetched for me."

"I'm beginning to believe," Lisa said to the sheriff, "that you are either a male chauvinist of the very worst kind, or even worse, part of the bunch I've had to deal with tonight. Either way, I've had way more than enough of you."

"That's too bad. I'm going to have to lock you up anyway. I still think there's a chance you're guilty of anywhere from three to five counts of murder. Depending of course, on who lives or dies."

"All the evidence points the other way," Mack told him, "so there'll be no arresting my wife tonight."

"I say there is, and there's no way to stop me from doing my duty."

"Other than break your damn neck," an even angrier Roy said, pushing his face tight into the sheriff's. "So back the hell off, or that's exactly what I intend to do to you."

"That's all I'm going to take from you. You're all under arrest."

Mack shrugged, shook his head, and told the sheriff, "Given what you're trying to do, I have no doubts that you're part of the human trafficking bunch that's been operating here. So, I'm arresting you."

"I won't allow you to do that to me."

"Too bad, but right now, there's not a damn thing you can do about it." He used his phone to call the state police.

They were lucky, and the patrolman who arrived was someone Mack had worked with in the past. He also knew Lisa, and admired all that she'd managed to accomplish in her short time in law enforcement. When he was told the situation he surprised everyone by laughing.

He turned to the Sheriff Tod Mcintire. "I think," he said, literally sneering at him, "that you are way past due getting your fat head out of your ass. It's a damn sight more likely that one of the many cows, out in pasture around here, is going to jump over the moon, then it is that Lisa murdered anyone. If there's dead men and she killed them, it was only because they needed killing. Not to mention, Jackstone county's been one we've been suspicious of harboring people involved in human trafficking for a while now."

The sheriff shook his head. "Her story still seems a bit too bazaar for me. But I guess I'll have to take your word for it. And I don't think what she did to the chief was quite necessary."

After sighing heavily, Lisa took the time to give him a full explanation about the knife and why she had it with her, even though she'd only planned to do some dancing.

She ended it with, "He was the second man within hours who tried to rape me. He was on top of me when I cut him. At the time, I wasn't much concerned where. As it's turned out though, I think what he lost is more than appropriate."

"Yeah, but, how would you like it if someone did something like that to you?"

"What a lot of men just like him did to me a long time ago," she said, thinking about her loss of the ability to have children, "was a lot worse. And if that worthless piece of garbage survives, I hope he suffers a lot all the years he lives."

"That's pretty harsh."

"No," Mack said, "It's not. Men who do what he was doing, dealing in human trafficking, only deserve the worst punishment we can give them. As far as I'm concerned, what she did wasn't only okay. It was proper and just, and I personally would love to see all men who do what he was doing, get that or similar treatment."

"You people are sure a bunch of hard asses," the sheriff complained.

Before they could carry the argument any further, a badly shaken deputy returned. He was so shaken he didn't notice all the vehicles parked there. He started talking even before he got all the way in the door.

"I tried calling you chief..." he started to say, but before he could finish Lisa stepped in front of him.

"Remember me?" she asked.

"What're you doing out here? You were locked in the cell."

"Guess what," she said. "I'm not locked in the cell anymore." She moved in tight against him, forcing him against the wall. He tried to edge away from her but couldn't. She was stronger than him and had little trouble controlling him. "Now you're going to tell all these people here what you found where you just were."

That's when the ambulance finally arrived. When the two men from it came in and saw the chief, they were shocked. Because they were professionals, they quickly overcame their shock and went to work on him. Once they had him stabilized, one of the men said to the other, "We really should find his penis. They might be able to reattach it."

Lisa couldn't resist. "It's over there," she pointing to the mangled piece of flesh.

"What the happened to it?" one of the men asked.

"Been a lot of traffic through here," she told them.

"And the cow just jumped over the moon," Sheriff Tod Mcintire mocked.

Lisa ignored him and turned again to the deputy. "Ready to talk?" she asked again.

He was and did. He first claimed he didn't want to do what he'd done, claiming the chief forced him to do it. Then he went on to describe what he'd found at the farm where Darrin took Lisa. One of the first things he said was that Darrin was among the dead.

The young man from the state police called it in and requested that someone be sent there to check it out. Lisa, Mack and Roy were then questioned for the next couple of hours by various members of the state police.

At the same time, they interviewed the four girls, who verified much of what Lisa told them. It was early morning before they were satisfied enough to let the three of them go.

They got home just in time to join the rest of the family for breakfast. And even though they were exhausted, they were hungry. Ben took extra care cooking their food, so when he set it in front of them, everything was done to perfection.

"So," Ben finally asked, "what's next?"

"If you're asking about the problems with Heavenly Homes, and Dell Whitcomb," Mack answered, "as far as I'm concerned, we are at war."

"And war is hell," Lisa added.

"We decided on the way home," Mack explained, "that Paul Danielson and I are going to spend whatever time is needed to catch the home's people doing something we can hang them for."

"And I'm going to work with much of the department," Lisa said, "doing as much research as possible on human trafficking. It seems to us, now that we've rescued two groups of girls, to be a far more serious problem here in Minnesota than we thought. I know we can't stop it all, but we've got to stop as much as we can."

"Looks like you've got your hands full," Ben said.

"We do," Mack answered, "but that seems to be a way of life now. I'm not surprised though. I knew life was going to come to this as soon as I found out about the plans to turn the refuge into a resort. So, it's been one thing after another for all the years since it was started."

"That it has," Roy agreed. "And back then, you picked up on what the future would bring quicker and better than anyone."

"I remember," Wanda said. "When he first told me what he thought, I was sure he was all wrong about it. Turned out, he was right, and I was all wrong."

"Seems like that's been true way too much over these last few years," Ben said, "When things go really wrong, it's all too often because someone wouldn't listen to Mack."

Mack just lowered his shaking head as he listened to a chorus of agreements to Ben's words. He appreciated what they were saying about him, but knew that it was only a small help for what was wrong with the world. Since he became a deputy, he'd learned that people didn't listen to what he and people like him had to say for a simple reason. If they did, they might have to change some small part in the way they lived. That, he knew, few people were willing to do.

CHAPTER 34

Dell Whitcomb felt totally frustrated by the recent events. His brother, the man he counted on for support with the nursing home business, was now dead. Along with too many other men involved in the lucrative human trafficking business. And Lisa and Mack Thomas were both still alive. A situation he found untenable.

They, more than anyone, were the cause of his problems. Whenever the law was involved in either enterprise, no matter the reason, either one or both of them was always had something to do with it.

As if that wasn't enough, because of the constant setbacks, the top management was leaning on him even harder than ever to bring an end to their constant interference. They would provide the money, they said, but it was up to him to find and hire the person or persons needed to accomplish the task.

The amount of money provided was extremely generous compared to what the standard fee was for that type of job. It proved that even the upper management of the Heavenly Homes Corporation was aware of how serious their problem had become.

The search for the right person soon became common knowledge among the criminal element in Clayborne and surrounding counties. Dell hoped to keep it contained. Because he didn't know how life worked outside his small world, his efforts ended in total failure. In less than two days, Lisa and Mack were aware of Dell's attempts to hire someone.

"Nothing much new there," Mack said to Lisa when they learned what Dell was trying to do.

"No, there isn't," she agreed. "But you'd think they might learn someday."

"When there's money involved, they're unable to use common sense. If they ran their business the way anyone equipped with any kind of human decency would, they could be expanding a reasonably profitable business now. Instead, they're forcing people into their horrible homes, which they run short staffed because their pay rates are too low, and they're still greedy for even more. While they're doing that, they don't care a damn who gets hurt. Their patients, members of law enforcement, or the public in general."

"I know, Mack. Compared to what they started with, we started Places Of Refuge on a shoestring. Yet, here we are, finding it easy to compete with them. Better yet, we're growing faster than they are."

Mack smiled at her last comment. "Yes, it's really something the way our company has taken off. When we started, I never would have believed we'd get far enough to turn it over to someone else so soon."

"Me either. I wonder how Wanda is doing in her search for someone to take over the company?"

She was doing exceptionally well actually. At the same time Mack and Lisa were talking about their company, Places Of Refuge, Wanda was negotiating the turnover of the company with a management group from a large, reputable, nonprofit organization. It was a company involved in the health care field for a very long time.

"So," commented the leader of the group, "you're telling us that all you and your partners want or plan to take out of the business is the equivalent of what you initially invested."

"That's right," she told the group. "But that is based on you signing a long-term contract stating the fact that you will continue to run the company as we have. The patients always come first, no matter their income, skin color, religion, or lack thereof, gender, or other imperfections. In order to provide the proper service to them, you'll need a large, well trained work force, that is paid a decent wage. All facilities will at all times be properly maintained. Finally, the entire company, including all accounting records, will be open to our inspection at all times. If you fail to follow these standards, the company will be subject to forfeiture."

"We whole heartedly agree with all that you requested regarding the standards you want us to maintain. But I still find it hard to believe none of you want any profit from Places Of Refuge."

Wanda then took the time to tell them how and why they started the business, and why it grew so big so fast. She finished with, "So you can see why we neither need nor want to profit from it. Our only wish is that it continues to serve all those people out there who often desperately need those services."

"You are a rare bunch, Wanda," the man said. "But a bunch everyone of us here are proud and pleased to work with. Now, how soon would you like to complete our transaction?"

"Yesterday," Wanda answered, her voice telling them she was serious. "It's been an honor for me to serve as CEO of our company, but not one I want to continue. I want to go back to my life of working with my husband, our cattle, and all the other things the Thomas family might get involved in."

"But won't you miss the power and control you have now. Not to mention the salary you must be drawing."

"Truth is, I don't much like being the boss. And as for the money, I've never taken a salary. I figured that money could better be spent to help the company expand so it could assist more people."

"Unreal. I'd guess then, Wanda, it would be a waste of time to ask you to continue in your current position?"

"You have got that one exactly right."

"What about your assistant? Would she be interested in the job?"

"I don't know. Let's ask her."

They brought Sue into the meeting. They let her sit down and relax before they asked her the question and told her what her salary and benefits would be.

"That's certainly a lot of money. Given the whole package you're offering me, it's more money than I ever dreamed of making." She sighed, gave them a big smile, and said, "But I have to turn you down. I've loved my time here, working with Wanda and sometimes other members of the Thomas family, but it's time to move on."

"But why," she was asked, "would you turn us down if you loved it while you were here?"

"A lot of it is because with Wanda gone, I wouldn't love it as much. She's been a great boss. I don't want to be the boss. That's just not my calling in life. So, with no disrespect intended, I plain don't want the job."

"I have to admit, not keeping either one of you is a letdown, but we are willing to move ahead with the deal anyway. One request though. Will one of you be willing to stay on and train the new CEO?"

"We'll both stay for two weeks after the turnover," Wanda said.

"That'll be great," the man said. "Unless anyone has any questions, we have a deal."

There were no questions at this meeting. That, however, wasn't the case at breakfast the next morning.

Mack had the first question. "I still will have the authority to represent Places Of Refuge if I need it to help out someone, won't I?"

"As long as you're a deputy sheriff, you will have it," Wanda said.

"Good," Mack said, then looked at Sue. "I assume you are leaving the company too?"

"I am. Like Wanda, I want to get back the life I had before."

"Before you do, is it possible I can hire you for one more job. I'll pay you the same salary you made at the company."

"Mack, you know I didn't draw a salary there."

Mack handed her a check. "I know, but none of us lost any money on it, so neither will you. This check will be covered when we make the final settlement with the nonprofit group, so you have to take it. You earned it."

She looked at the amount. "My god," she said, "this is too much."

"No, it isn't. So don't argue. Just tell me, will you do one more job for all of us?"

"I can tell by the look on your face, Mack," she answered, "that there's something devious in that question."

"You're right. But it isn't all bad. It just might be a bit difficult. Maybe even a little bit more than what would be called simply difficult."

"That sounds almost depressing. What kind of horrible thing do you want me to do?"

"I want you to deal with a couple of old relics. What you'll have to do will be loaded with a lot of positives and negatives. The thing is, you are one of the few people I know of who has the talents needed to get the job done."

"I don't know if I should take that as a compliment or run and hide. So, before I decide to do the latter, you'd best come out and tell me what it is you really want."

"I know this is going to sound scary, but please consider who all you're going to be doing this for."

"Come out with it, Mack."

"Okay. I want you to make these two old men sitting at this table computer literate."

Sue opened her mouth in shock, then shook her head in disbelief. "Do you have any idea what you're asking, Mack?"

"A lot, I know."

"That's enough of that kind of talk," Ben complained. "We can't be as bad as that."

"We for damn sure aren't," Roy added.

Sue couldn't help it. She laughed. It was infectious, and soon they were all laughing. As it died, she said, "I'll give it a try, Mack. But I won't guaranty the results. That'll be entirely up to them. And I'll need a couple of backup computers, so when they screw theirs up, the lessons won't have to stop."

So, it was agreed, starting the next day, Ben and Roy would enter a world they knew little to nothing about.

CHAPTER 35

Concerned as he was about the fact that Heavenly Homes had put a price on his and Lisa's heads, Mack still took the time to join a morning class in the refuge. As the students slowly walked one of the original trails with their instructor, Mack was impressed by how much they'd already learned. He was even more impressed by how much more they seemed to want to learn.

Their reaction toward the destruction caused by the fire differed from most people. Rather than dwell on it, they were far more interested in the way the land and the life it contained was recovering. They constantly pointed out new growth that appeared since their last lesson, along with the plants they'd studied before and that were now reaching maturity.

He was equally impressed in their newly acquired ability to identify many of the plants. He loved the way they got excited whenever they saw any kind of animal life, be it anything from a butterfly to a herd of deer.

As much as he appreciated the good the lessons were doing for the students, seeing the recovery take place among the ruins from the fire did wonders for his spirit. Given all the danger and misery he and Lisa had recently been through, being out and about where life made sense was something he very much needed.

He somehow managed to stay with the group for a little over an hour before his cell phone rang. A carload of teenagers was involved in a serious accident on the four lane highway, just north of Kingsburg. All available deputies were requested to assist at the scene.

When Mack got there, he found both north bound lanes blocked. The car with the teenagers had apparently drifted off the road, hit a guard rail, swerved back on the highway, where it rolled over several times. Two of the six boys inside were killed, and the other four were seriously injured.

Three ambulances and many law enforcement people were already on hand, so about all Mack could do was assist with traffic control. The person who'd taken charge of that detail sent Mack back down the highway, where he'd be the first person a driver going north on the highway would see.

Mack had seen and worked at the scene of more accidents than he wanted to remember, so he knew well what to do. It all went okay until a heavy-set man driving a shiny new pickup decided he didn't need to pay any attention to Mack's directions. When he tried to drive around Mack, he stepped in front of the truck.

"Get the hell out of my way," the man screamed.

Mack held up both hands, palms facing out, telling the man to stop. This time the man got out of his truck.

"I don't know who it is you think you are," he said, looking Mack up and down, "but you damn sure got no business playing out here in the traffic. So, one more time, get the hell out of my way or I'll have to move you."

"No," Mack answered, keeping his voice as even as he could. "Either you get back in your truck, or I'll be forced to arrest you."

"The hell you will. You ain't nothing but a play cowboy with a toy badge," the man yelled, referring to Mack's clothes.

"Sorry," Mack said, "but the badge is real, and I can and will arrest you if you can't behave. Your behavior is putting people at risk, and that's something I can't allow."

"I'll show you what you can allow." The man took a swing at Mack, who easily ducked out of the way.

"You don't want to play that game," Mack warned him.

By then, a few other drivers were out of their cars, watching the action. It was action that was short lived. When the man took a second swing at him, Mack was left with no choice. He grabbed the man's arm, twisted it behind him, then quickly cuffed him.

Most of the crowd gathered around them were surprised by Mack's moves. They all fully expected a knockdown, drag out fight. Only a few understood the wisdom of Mack's method of dealing with the man. The rest were mostly disappointed with the lack a serious fight.

Mack quickly got the attention of a highway patrolman who'd just arrived on the scene, and he carted the man away for Mack.

The next couple of hours went somewhat smoother for Mack, who stayed with the traffic detail until the accident scene was cleaned up. He was just getting into his own pickup to leave when the driver of a speeding car panicked when a highway patrolman pulled out onto the highway. The driver slammed on his brakes, went into an uncontrolled slide, and slammed into the guardrail. The car slid another fifty feet before coming to a stop.

The driver wasn't seriously injured, but the accident kept Mack directing traffic for over another hour before the mess on the highway was cleaned up. He was thoroughly tired of dealing with highway traffic by the time he left the scene.

Tired or not, he felt a deep-down sense of satisfaction from the time he spent at the accident. It was a relatively simple task that he performed, but one that was necessary. By doing it, he knew he'd made the lives of a lot of people on the highway much safer that day. It seemed to him that it was time well spent.

When he picked up Lisa at the sheriff's office at the end of the day, he told her how he felt about the time he spent at the accident.

"I understand what you mean," she said. "It often seems, on this job, that it's the small things we do that are the most satisfying."

"As horrible as accidents so often are, being able to help when they happen does make what we do worth something."

The trouble was their good feelings didn't Last. As they turned onto the road that ran passed their driveway, a shot rang out. The bullet smashed through the windshield, between them. Mack slammed the truck into the ditch, turning it so his side of the truck was facing the direction the shot came from.

"Get down on the floor and stay there," he ordered Lisa.

This time she did as she was told. But at the same time, she told him, "You get the hell down too."

He did, just as another bullet penetrated the driver's side window. "I think we'll be better off out of here and on your side of the truck."

"Me too," she agreed.

Lisa opened the door and stayed low as she slid out. Mack followed her, then slowly stood up enough to see in the direction the bullets were coming from.

It took a moment for his eyes to focus on the landscape in front of him. As they did, he saw a man climb out of a large oak tree. He had a rifle in his hand, which slowed his escape. That didn't help Mack any. The man was too far away for him to try a shot. A pistol just wasn't accurate at that distance.

The best Mack could do under the circumstances was to mentally note the make and color of the car. He and Lisa got back in his truck, and he took out after it, but the car had too much of a head start. He knew he'd lost it before he travelled three miles. Even so, he had little doubt about who was responsible for the sniper.

Heavenly Homes was behind it, and he already had a plan on how to get the man who actually did the shooting, along with the person who hired him. Capturing the people who were ultimately responsible, which was the Heavenly Homes top management, was going to be a far more difficult task.

As soon as Mack stopped and turned around to head for home, Lisa said, "I can tell from the look on your face, Mack, that you've already got some kind of idea about this. What are you planning?"

"Nothing elaborates, that's for sure."

"I didn't expect it to be. Not this quick. But I know it's something, so tell me, what is your plan?"

"Simple. You have to agree, Heavenly Homes is behind this. So, I'm going after them, tonight."

"How?"

"To start with, a stakeout. All night. I think there's a chance the guy doing the shooting today is going to need some help finding a place to stay. I don't think he'll want to go far. He'll want to stay around so he can get another shot at us."

"Are you sure? If I was him, I'd be long gone already."

"If he was a real pro, he probably would be. At least temporarily. This guy isn't a pro. Given where he was shooting from, he shouldn't have missed. Hitting either one of us wasn't that difficult. He missed both times."

"But why are you going to stake out Heavenly Homes?"

"He's going to know that we'll be checking out any and all motels in or near Kingsburg. So there's a chance he's going to want to have a meeting with Dell Whitcomb to work something out. The logical place for that is the home."

"Wouldn't they know that we might suspect them of doing that?"

"You'd think so, but neither one of them is likely to ever have a bubble that will reach plumb or level, so there's a good chance they won't. Not in the middle of the night anyway."

"What time do you plan to start your stakeout?"

"A couple of hours after dark. Even then, I expect it'll be a bit of a wait."

"I suppose you think you're going to do it alone?"

"Well, sure. How else would I do it?"

"With help."

"I don't really need any, and there's no one I'd ask to do it."

"Why not?"

"If for no other reason then it's boring. There's also a chance it could get dangerous."

"I'm aware of that. And that's why I'm asking about you doing it alone."

"I know, Lisa, but I still don't want to drag someone else into it, especially since this is just a hunch of mine. I've got no proof."

"Maybe not, but you do have someone to go with you."

"Who?"

"God, you can be so dense sometimes. You've got me. I'm going to be there next to you tonight."

"I can't let you do that. You're the sheriff. You've got to be at work tomorrow."

"And if I'm late in the morning, and tired after I get there? What's going to happen? Is someone going to fire me? Besides, that's not why you don't want my help. You're being overprotective again."

"No, I'm not, Lisa."

"Yes, you are. I'm going with tonight. We'll take my truck. Its windows aren't full of holes."

"What if I tell you no?"

"You can't. I'm the sheriff. I'm your boss. More than that, I'm your wife, so you have to let me do what I want."

"You're also too damn stubborn for your own good."

"Maybe. But I am going."

Mack gave up then, and they went the rest of the way home in silence. On the way, Mack decided to take a shower right away, then a short nap before they started the stakeout.

Moments after he stepped under the hot water, the shower doors opened. Lisa joined him.

"What brings you in here?" he asked, the grin on his face obvious.

"You, Mack," she said, her face filled with serious. "I'm here for you. I hope you'll except what I'm offering."

"Except it hell. I'm taking it."

She smiled then.

CHAPTER 36

It was close to two AM when Dell Whitcomb drove into the private parking lot at the back of Heavenly Homes main building. Mack and Lisa were both tired by then, but instantly came to life when they saw him.

They were parked in the public parking lot, but in a spot near the side of the building where they could see the private lot. The parking lot lights didn't quite cover the entire lot, so their parking spot was relatively dark. It made it difficult to see them sitting inside Lisa's pickup.

And that's why the man who tried to kill them didn't see them, even though he carefully looked around the lot before leaving his car. As they planned, they let him get far enough away to have his back to them before they left the truck.

As quiet as they could, they moved up on him, but waited for him to start opening the heavy back door before they made their move on him. Lisa managed to get so close to him that she had her gun touching the back of his head before they said anything.

"Hands on top of your head," Mack ordered.

Instead of following his command, the man spun around, hoping to grab Lisa's gun. She was too quick for him, and ducked out of his way, then slapped him upside the head with her gun as she came back up. It left a nice bruise.

"Try that again," she said, "and I promise I'll hurt you. A lot."

Mack quickly put the cuffs on him, then turned to Lisa. "You're the boss," he told her, "so you get to be the one to call the troops. No point in going after Dell without plenty of backup. I'm sure he's got some goons on duty no matter what time it is."

'I expect so," she agreed.

They weren't at all sure their idea about Dell and there would be sniper were going to actually meet, so they hadn't put anyone on standby. That meant it took a while for their backup to arrive. Three deputies arrived in separate cars. Two men and one woman. Everyone wanted to go in after Dell, and no one wanted to stay outside with the prisoner.

Because she was the sheriff, Lisa felt she should take the lead, and volunteered to stay with the prisoner.

"All of you," she said to them before they went in, "be careful in there. And watch your backs."

Mack took the lead going in. He led the group directly to Dell's office. To his and everyone's surprise, he wasn't there. It meant they needed to start searching for him.

At the same time, Dell had no idea what was going on. When his man didn't show at the time he was expected, Dell grew restless, and started roaming through the halls. Doing so, he thought about all the old ladies available to him. He'd committed several rapes since the first one and was now addicted to them.

As he passed the room of a cute little lady, who was definitely senile, he decided that it couldn't hurt anything to try her out. If he somehow missed the man he was supposed to meet, so be it. It wasn't Dell who needed help. So, he entered the room. She was in one of the beds next to a wall.

He didn't do anything other than stare at her at first. Then he slowly eased the blanket covering her off. Now that he'd raped so many of them, he liked the way they looked. It quickly excited him as he watched her. He opened his pants and made himself ready to do it to her.

She was younger than any of the others, and was there because her dementia was so serious, not because of physical disabilities. So, when he woke her up as he tried lifting her hospital gown out of the way, she resisted him.

Dell was shocked when she slapped his hands away. None of the others ever did anything to stop him. He was always sure they didn't fight him because they didn't mind so much what he did. He was too dense to realize they didn't fight him only because they weren't able to.

It was different this time. This lady could fight back, and she did it with all the strength of a fifty-five year old woman. Because she'd only been in the home for a couple of days, she hadn't yet suffered the physical degradation that came from lack of exercise and an inadequate diet.

He persisted with his attempts to control her. He knew he should stop, but her resistance was arousing him to the point he couldn't think beyond controlling, then raping her.

She was too strong. She just continued fighting him. Finally, she screamed. No one had ever done that. He was enraged and slapped her face several times. She continued to fight and scream, so he hit her with his fist. She slowed her resistance, but continued to scream. He moved her pillow over her head.

As he put pressure on it to stop her breathing, deputy sheriff Patricia Newman barged into the room. She pulled out her weapon, and yelled, "Stop! Stop it now." A now crazed Dell ignored her. "She yelled again. He still paid no attention. Knowing she had no choice, the deputy shot him. He was sideways to her, so when the bullet entered his shoulder and missed the bone, it traveled into his chest.

At the same time Dell landed on the floor, one of the other deputies entered the room. He ran over to check on Dell, but momentarily pulled back when he saw what was hanging out from his pants. It was obvious what Dell's plans for the woman were. He hesitated for a moment, wondering if he cared whether the bleeding was stopped or not. After some soul searching, he went ahead and did what he could.

Patricia called 911 to get an ambulance as she moved to check on the lady in the bed, who was far more angry than injured. She didn't understand who was who or what was what, so she began a long stream of curses, damning everyone in the room, along with most of the rest of the world.

Patricia smiled, relieved that the woman was unharmed. She knew that if she'd been slower, she could as easy as not be dead now.

Mack soon joined them. After Patricia and the other deputy told him what happened, he told her, "You did the right thing. Even if you would've killed him, it would still be the right thing.

When the crew from the ambulance finished treating Dell, they picked him up on the stretcher to carry him out to the ambulance. He was dazed from the bullet wound and now drugged, but he managed to complain anyway.

"Damn bitch. Fighting with me. None of the others ever fought with me. Damn bitch."

The only thing Mack wondered about was whether or not Dell would have raped the women after she was dead. Mack guessed yes. He then told the deputy who wasn't at all involved in the shooting to go out and relieve Lisa from guarding the prisoner, and send her in.

As soon as she heard the explanation of what happened, just as Mack did, she told Patricia she'd done the right thing.

"I only did my job," Patricia answered. "I didn't want to shoot him, but he didn't give me any choice."

"Like I already told you," Lisa said, "You did the right thing. So don't worry about it. The shooting was totally justified. If he wouldn't have been trying to kill her, he would have been raping her."

Because of the shooting, it took the rest of the night to complete the initial investigation. When it ended, Mack and Lisa went to Katy's Kafe for breakfast. It was too late in the morning to eat with the family.

"I'm glad," Mack told her after they were seated at their table, "that you were outside when Patricia caught Dell."

"Why? Don't you think I could have handled it?"

Mack chuckled at her sarcasm. "I think you could have handled both arrests on your own. I doubt you would have wounded Dell, but I have no doubts about your ability to handle the situation tonight. I'm glad you were out of the picture because you don't need to be investigated for another shooting right now."

"I could handle it if I had too."

"I know. I just think, that right now, it's better if you don't have to. I think we have enough to do and to worry about without that. Besides, I'd like it if you and I could find some extra alone time."

"And if we do, Then what?"

"Mostly just enjoy the time we have together. There are no better times than those I spend with you."

Lisa tried not to let him see how deeply his words affected her, but she failed miserably when her eye's filled with tears. Even with a smile on her face.

"I love you too," She said, as she reached across the table and took his hand. When the waitress came to take their order, she was still holding it. It took them a moment before they were aware of her presence.

CHAPTER 37

It was a day Lisa waited for, for months. Dale and Kathy were home, and this was the day he was returning to work. When he walked into the office he was met with applause, which surprised him. He would have been even more surprised if he'd known that Lisa was the one leading it.

She greeted him with a big hug, Mack with a handshake. "Good to have you back," they both told him.

"Good to be back," he smiled. "Difficult as it is at times, it's still easier to be sheriff than it is following a famous singer around the world."

"That might have been true when you left," Mack said, "but after what Lisa's been through since she's been sheriff, she might argue that."

"Is that why you didn't try to keep the job, Lisa? Because of how tough it was? You're well-liked and respected enough you know, to have kept it if you wanted it."

"I didn't quit because it was hard. I quit because you're a better sheriff than I am."

"Not according to what the county commissioners have to say about it. According to them, you solved more crimes in the short time you were sheriff than anyone else ever has."

"If that's true, which I doubt, it's only because there was more crime while you were gone than normal. Either way, I don't want to be sheriff. I'm Mack Thomas's wife, and he's been one hell of an influence on me. Rather than be sheriff, I want to be out and about everyday doing what I can to help. I also love riding solo when I'm out there. I can make my own decisions when there's trouble, and not have to concentrate on the safety and needs of someone riding with me."

Dale turned to Mack. "How do you feel about it. Are you going to be okay with her out there alone, everyday?"

"I don't have a choice, Dale. I can't tell her no because having her out there alone scares me. When I'm out there, it scares her every bit as much. And she's more than proven that she can handle herself, protect herself, as well as anyone else. Including you and me."

"I know she can. But she's still a female, and it's in our blood to think we have to protect her. Because of that, I worry more about how you're going to deal with it, than I am about how she's going to handle it."

"It's going to be okay, Dale. Lisa and it have worked it out between us. When the day comes, she needs someone to cover her back, which it sometimes will, I'll be there to do it. More important, she's now able to accept my being there when it's necessary. The same way I am when she covers my ass."

"That's good to hear. So now I guess I better get to work and earn the great big paycheck I get twice a month."

Mack laughed. "It's still a lot bigger than mine."

"True. But even with the money Kathy's making now, you still have a hell of a lot more of it than I do.'

Dale left them then and went into his office. An office Lisa had put back almost exactly the way it was before he took his six-month sabbatical. He signed heavily when he sat in his chair. He loved being sheriff, but at the same time, envied Mack and Lisa. There always was and always would be a part of him that equally loved the freedom of spending his days riding solo out and about in the community.

And that's exactly what they were about to do as they left the sheriff's office and walked to their vehicles. They both drove black, Ford F250s, equipped with everything a deputy sheriff could possibly need. Everything, that is, that had so far been invented.

Lisa decided to drive through Kingsburg first. Mack left for the far reaches of the county. They were in their own element now, and happy to be there.

Epilogue

A thorough investigation of the Heavenly Homes facility in Kingsburg was started after Dell and his would-be sniper/killer were arrested. Several of his goons who were supposed to be support people were found to have serious criminal records. There were warrants out for some of them.

With further digging and interviews of the female patients, the large number of rapes was finally discovered. It was also confirmed that the DNA from the semen found in one of the three women murdered months before belonged to Dell Whitcomb. He was charged with their murders.

Some of the male caregivers were charged with rape. All of the rest of the management team from the Kingsburg Heavenly Homes were arrested for some crime or another.

All the financial information that Sue had gathered about all of Heavenly homes was leaked to the press. Because of that information, along with the severity of the various crimes, the state took over the home, along with several others in the state. They still needed managing though, and a deal was negotiated with the group now in control of Places Of Refuge.

After taking control, they quickly changed the mode of operation, and where possible, transferred many patients to Places Of Refuge facilities. It gave those patients a better home and eased the crowding at Heavenly Homes.

The media, having the financial information, and having discovered the rest of the scandal, made it the lead in the news for a whole day. That was enough to bring about several investigations in several states. About half the Heavenly Homes investigated were confiscated, all of which were put under Places Of Refuge management.

Judge Mathew A Barker, who escaped to Mexico, was living quite well. He had two Mexican girls living with him. He consistently did with them whatever his latest whim required. They, in turn, had little choice but to allow it. They both came from large families who never had enough money for a decent life. The girls made enough from the judge to offer considerable help.

The main way the girls found to cope with the judge, a man they soundly hated, was the heavy use of drugs. Because of that, drug dealers were frequent visitors to his rather luxurious home.

The girls frequently engaged in sexual activities with those dealers, as it proved to be a nice boost in their income. It was something that was working fine until the Judge caught them. He went into a rage.

He was, however, a rather puny man compared to the dealer he attacked. It was a bad move on his part. He died from a knife wound.

In the latest election Minnesota did what it occasionally does and voted liberal. The elected Democrats wasted no time in getting rid of the special task force. Rather than help anyone not rich, it had proved to be more of a vigilante mob than a task force to assist people who genuinely needed help.

In doing so, they brought up loud cries from the political right, especially people like Jason Johnson. For him, losing his place on the task force was even more devastating than losing his job at Heavenly Homes. He was not at all prepared for the loss of both of his jobs and quickly ran out of money. Because he was rather incompetent at nearly everything, he quickly found himself out on the street. Within three days of homelessness, he had a nervous breakdown.

He was eventually taken to a hospital, where he was ruled mentally ill. He is now a resident of Heavenly Homes, where he spends his days in a hallway, sitting in a wheelchair, wearing a straight jacket.

Sue Sartor shook her head in exasperation one more time as she tried to explain to Roy why the computer wasn't doing what he expected. She once again pointed out that he'd skipped three steps on his search for the results he wanted.

"You know," he complained to her, "I've always thought you women were hard to understand. Compared to these damn machines, you are all easy."

"What do you mean, Roy? Easy to understand, or just easy?"

Roy smiled. "Don't go there, Sue. We both know there's nothing easy about you. There's too much of you, too much about you, to ever be easy."

"I'm glad you think so," she smiled, "but you're married, and your wife is my best friend, so forget all the eases and concentrate on the computer."

"I'll try. You're right, I am married. And to a far better person than an old man like me deserves. But all that said, you'll never hear me complain about having you be the one who's trying to teach me all this crap."

It was heart breaking for Dave and Elaine to watch her. The past few weeks had been difficult to see and to do what needed doing. Jill had been going steadily downhill for a couple of years, but suddenly the process of dying had sped up considerably. She could no longer move much beyond her fingers or blink her eyes. Even swallowing was difficult for her.

As the hospice people, who visited every day now, told them, it was all part of the dying process. Feeding her became impossible, and the only moisture she got was from a tiny sponge on the end of plastic stick.

She stayed in that condition for a week, until that fateful day she didn't wake up. She was laying partially on her side, and moaned in pain when they tried to move her on her back and straighten her legs.

Luckily, the nurse who came that morning managed to do it while causing Jill a minimum of pain. All they could do now was try to keep her comfortable. Every two hours she got a small doze of morphine from an eyedropper under her tongue to control the pain. Other drugs to help to her swallow and to breath were given the same way.

On the evening of the third day of her coma, Dave and Elaine were with her when her breathing became extremely labored. Dave held her hand, and Elaine rested her own hand on Jill's leg. They stood there like that for a few minutes. Then Dave felt a light squeeze of his hand from Jill. He wondered if she was saying I love you, or if it was a simple goodbye. He looked at her, but she didn't appear to be aware of anything. A couple of minutes went by and she gasped for breath. It was her last one. She was dead.

Dave made the call to hospice, and they made all the other calls. Three hours later two people who seemed to Dave to be too young to be doing such a task, came and took her away.

It wasn't until they carried her out the door the enormity of it hit him. She was gone forever. He would never see her again. That's when he cried.

Sheriff Tod Mcintire brought the girls, one by one, up from the underground room they used for the holding room and loaded them into the van. The driver was young and was only used for the job because his skill behind the wheel was far superior to most people. The man riding shotgun was an old pro. He was a veteran of many battles, both with cops and rival criminal gangs.

They were leaving for a meeting on the east coast somewhere, where they would negotiate a price for the six girls they were hauling. They were relaxed about the trip. They'd already made five trips together, without incident, and didn't see any reason for concern this time.

As they drove away, the sheriff felt very pleased with himself. Prices for the girls were high, and he'd managed to capture them on a regular basis, in spite of the onetime interference from the law enforcement people over in Clayborne County. People he still wanted to be rid of.

It was early morning when Mack left the bed. Lisa woke up as he did. "What's wrong, Mack? Why are you up already?"

"I'm not sure. Just kind of restless. I think I'll go take a short walk in the refuge. Maybe that'll bring back my balance. Right now, I feel a bit off kilter. Why don't you go back to sleep until I get back?"

"Okay, Mack, but you be careful out there. You never know what you might run into in the dark." She was sleeping again by the time he left the house.

It was still a while before sunrise when he started his walk on an old hiking trail, but enough first light to see where he was walking. There was a slight chill in the air, but it didn't bother Mack any. It was outside, fresh, clean air, and that's what he loved.

As he moved deeper into the refuge and the light grew stronger, he began to see ever more plant life. One of the first things he noticed was a wild grape vine crawling up the trunk of a tree killed by the fire.

Wild grasses had expanded and covered more ground in the two weeks since his last walk. It took more light before he could see the colors of the flowers of the many blooming plants. Trees that survived were now fully leafed out, and the general feel of the land around him was a world very much alive.

He'd seen deer on the outer edges of the burned out refuge on past walks, but today he saw a herd of seven deer deep into the refuge. That meant food for them was already being produced.

Once the sun was up and he had full light, he often watched various small critters out and about doing their daily chores. For the first time since the fire, a large bull snake moved out of a clump of tall grass, and seemingly without fear, crossed the path he was on just inches from his feet. As they do to most humans, the sudden appearance of the snake shocked Mack. Strong enough so he felt like his heart stopped for a moment. As he recovered, he felt a sense of wonder at the sight of it.

Snakes were a creature all too often damned and hated by people. The fact they were as beneficial to humans as they are, never seemed to matter. Mack strongly suspected the mythology in the bible about Eve and the snake had a lot to do with it.

The rest of his walk was filled with the wonders of the natural world and he arrived home feeling refreshed and ready to take on whatever it was the world was going to hand him.

Lisa was in the kitchen when he went inside the house. She was dressed in her deputy's uniform, had her hair back in a bun, and no makeup on.

He stopped and stared at her. "What's wrong?" she asked when he did.

He smiled, moved his head back and forth a couple of times, then said, "And I thought it was beautiful out there. It didn't compare."

She smiled back at him. "I love you too."